S0-CFX-248

POSSESS ME

POSSESS ME

K. R. Alexander

Scholastic Inc.

If you purchased this book without a cover, you should be aware that this book is stolen property. It was reported as "unsold and destroyed" to the publisher, and neither the author nor the publisher has received any payment for this "stripped book."

Copyright © 2022 by Alex R. Kahler writing as K.R. Alexander

All rights reserved. Published by Scholastic Inc., *Publishers since 1920.* SCHOLASTIC and associated logos are trademarks and/or registered trademarks of Scholastic Inc.

The publisher does not have any control over and does not assume any responsibility for author or third-party websites or their content.

No part of this publication may be reproduced, stored in a retrieval system, or transmitted in any form or by any means, electronic, mechanical, photocopying, recording, or otherwise, without written permission of the publisher. For information regarding permission, write to Scholastic Inc., Attention: Permissions Department, 557 Broadway, New York, NY 10012.

This book is a work of fiction. Names, characters, places, and incidents are either the product of the author's imagination or are used fictitiously, and any resemblance to actual persons, living or dead, business establishments, events, or locales is entirely coincidental.

ISBN 978-1-338-80739-4

10 9 8 7 6 5 4 3 2   22 23 24 25 26

Printed in the U.S.A.   40
First edition, November 2022

Book design by Keirsten Geise

For those who Know
precisely who they are.

6

The world is filled with hidden treasures. You just have to know where to look.

My friend Javier and I have spent our lives scouring every inch of Marshall Junction for oddities and collectibles. We've combed through garage sales and flea markets and pawnshops, poked around the woods and the parks, and even brought a metal detector down to the lake to see what we could find. Over the years, we've assembled quite the collection of rusted rings and neglected necklaces, discarded dice and creepy cameras. We even found a stuffed squirrel hidden in the trunk of a tree.

Really, if you're willing to look in strange places, there's no telling what treasures you might find.

But there's one place we never dared to go. The one place *no one* in the town dared to go.

At school, kids called it the Blood Manor.

It was built by an eccentric old woman in the middle of the woods, just outside town. Bigger and grander than any house in Marshall Junction, filled with artifacts she'd collected from all over the globe. Some said there were treasures in there that were stolen from kings and queens. Some said every artifact was cursed.

There were hundreds of rumors, but no one knew the truth. Because the old woman never let anyone past the high iron fence that surrounded the property.

There were other rumors, too. Rumors that kids had gone missing from town. Rumors that, at night, you could hear terrible noises coming from the Manor. Screams for help.

And then, in the middle of the night, it caught fire.

This was a long time ago, before I was even born. But my dad once told me: "Kaden, when that place burned, it burned green. And those fires didn't crackle and burn like normal fires. They screamed like the wails of the dead."

The house mostly survived, but no one else did. The owner was never found. Nor was there ever a confirmed cause for the fire. It was a mystery. One everyone in town was more than happy to forget.

Especially because, at night, rumor had it that people could still hear the owner hammering away, eternally building a house she'd never complete. Waiting for unsuspecting visitors she could trap inside her endless halls.

Most people have been too scared to enter. Or maybe they were too smart to take such a risk.

But I knew I had to go in.

I knew I would find artifacts that would make my own collection complete.

I just had no way of knowing that what I found would do everything in its power to unmake *me*.

1

"Check this out, Kaden!" Javier calls.

I look up from the pile of old coins I'd been sorting through to see my best friend hunched over an old dollhouse.

"What are you . . ." I mutter, but I drop the coins and walk over. I swear Mr. Hubbard hasn't gotten any new coins in since the Second World War. I don't even know why I bother.

I make it two steps over to Javier before he turns to face me.

I nearly yelp.

"What. In the world. Is that?" I ask.

Javier giggles and bounces his find up and down in front of him.

It's a mouse.

A small white taxidermy mouse. Standing on its hind legs. In a pink tutu. It even has a wand and a tiny pink crown.

"Isn't it cute?" he asks. He makes it twirl and dance in the air.

Javier and me, we're outcasts around here. Partly because of how we look (him, with his blue-streaked hair, tie-dyed shirts, me with my pastel wardrobe and sequined everything), but mostly because both of us are . . . weird. And we're both okay with that. We know who we are.

"No," I reply. "It's creepy. I mean, think about it: Who actually *made* that thing? Someone had to sew a tiny tutu and"—I look closer—"those are *rhinestones* on the tiara, dude. Who does that?"

Javier shrugs.

"Someone who has a lot of free time on their hands?" he offers. "And likes mice. And *The Nutcracker*. Oooh, we could collect a bunch of these and make an animatronic scene from *The*

Nutcracker. We could call it the 'Mice-capades.' Get it?"

I roll my eyes. "You're thinking of the *Ice* Capades," I say. "Totally different things."

"We can give it little ice skates," he counters. He swooshes the mouse around in front of me like it's doing some grand routine.

"You've had way too much sugar," I say.

"Maybe a little."

I raise my eyebrow.

"Okay, maybe like a lot. I didn't realize the extra-large sodas were going to be the size of buckets. Oh, also, do you think Mr. Hubbard will let me use his bathroom? I really have to pee."

Like you haven't gotten the extra-large sodas dozens of times before!

"Only for paying customers," I say. We've also gone over *this* a dozen times. I swear, he just drinks the extra-large sodas before coming here so he *has* to buy something.

He turns the mouse so it faces him and smiles at it.

"Looks like you're coming home with me!" he

says, and trots off to the front desk to pay and get the bathroom key.

I can't help it—I smile the moment his back is turned, and for a brief second let myself imagine creating a miniature mechanical diorama. I think I already have a few motors in my parents' garage, which I've turned into my own workshop. I definitely have some LEDs I could turn into stage lights.

I shake my head.

"No," I whisper to myself. "No way. We are *not* going to devote ourselves to taxidermy ice-skating mice."

The last time I let myself get distracted by one of Javier's wilder ideas, I ended up with six boxes of silly string and a toy train. Don't ask. I'm still trying to get rid of all the silly string.

For the last few years, Javier and I have been collecting an assortment of oddities. It currently takes up an entire wall of shelves in my room. But we don't collect just anything. We're looking for things that stand out, that tell a story. Some kids collect trading cards or figurines. I collect oddities. And if other kids or parents look at me strangely, well, that's their problem for being boring.

As I look around Mr. Hubbard's antique shop for the millionth time, I start to despair that we won't ever find anything remotely unique or interesting here.

I stroll past the dusty shelves, peering into glass cabinets filled with old jewelry that's tarnished beyond recognition. There are wooden boxes of tattered postcards, many of them with cursive sentences addressed to missed lovers or distant friends. I try not to read those. Even though the writers and recipients are probably long gone (and even though, yes, I have plenty of antiques that were surely personal), there's just something about reading someone's private life that feels wrong. Like, if a hundred years from now someone was selling my journal in a thrift store, I probably wouldn't want anyone else reading it, even if I didn't know they were doing it. I mean, it's personal. It's who I am.

Words are memory made permanent. They're important.

I pause in front of a jewelry box I haven't seen before and slowly open the lid.

"Just got that in last week," Mr. Hubbard says from beside me.

I nearly jump out of my skin.

"Very valuable," Mr. Hubbard continues. As though he doesn't realize he's scared me half to death. Which is highly possible, because Mr. Hubbard is extremely nearsighted. Every antique here still passes his scrutiny, but he can't see the customers so well.

"Oh?" I ask.

I open the jewelry box.

"Indeed," he replies. "Most of those rings are older than you."

I am twelve. This is an antiques store—that isn't hard to do. It sort of goes with the name.

I just nod, then pick up one of the rings and pretend to examine it. I can already tell that there isn't anything of interest in here. A few tarnished gold bands, some silver earrings, a string of pearls. Faded stamps, for some reason. This stuff could be valuable. It's just not valuable to me.

"Still think it's a little strange for you two to go rooting around in other people's things," he says in his grumbly voice. "Some might see it as meddling in other people's business."

Says the guy who owns an antiques store that only sells other people's business!

I don't say that, though. I hate confrontation, and I can't have the only peddler of strange things in this town come to hate me.

"We're very respectful," I reply instead.

"That's what Miss Hoffweller said, too. And look what happened to her."

The name is oddly familiar, but I swear I don't know anyone called Hoffweller.

Thankfully, I'm saved by Javier, who comes back with the ballet mouse held lovingly to his chest.

"Hey, Mr. Hubbard," Javier says. "Thanks for letting me use the bathroom. I wanted to ask—who donated Ferdinand?"

"Ferdinand?" I ask.

Javier holds up the mouse.

Of course.

"Strictly confidential," Mr. Hubbard says. He eyes us up and down. "Remember, kids: Meddling leads to trouble."

"We'll remember," Javier says. He looks to me. "Ready to go?"

I nod. "Did you . . . ?"

"Oh yeah, Ferdinand is all mine. Come on, little buddy. Adventure time!"

He heads toward the front door, making the mouse dance around as we go.

I follow close behind, glancing over my shoulder only once to see Mr. Hubbard standing by the jewelry box, his hands shaking slightly as he hovers them over the lid.

Something clicks.

Mr. Hubbard is a widower. I wonder if the box was his wife's.

My gut sinks with the thought, but then we're out in the bright, sticky Nebraska sun, and Javier is dancing around with Ferdinand while humming a waltz, and he looks so ridiculous I can't help but laugh.

He just smiles at me and goes back to dancing with his mouse.

We make our way down the street. Downtown is mostly deserted, a bunch of two-story joined buildings that are filled with more FOR RENT signs than there are shop signs. No one is on the street. No one here walks. Especially not in this heat.

"What are we doing tonight?" he asks. "Maybe video games and pool party at my house?"

"I'm in," I reply. "Just gotta text my parents."

They won't mind. I spend more time at Javier's than I do at my own house, especially in the summer. Because, pool.

Besides, there are only a few days of vacation left. My parents know I'd rather spend it with my best— and only—friend.

"Hey," I say as I text home. "Do you know a Miss Hoffweller?"

Javier may act like a big goof, but he actually pays very close attention, and his mind is like Alcatraz— once he's locked some trivia inside there, it's never getting out. We've both lived in this town our whole lives, but he definitely knows this place's history better than I do.

He stops immediately and asks, "What? Why?"

"Mr. Hubbard mentioned her. Said she used to collect a lot of weird stuff. Like us."

"She's nothing like us," he says.

"Why?"

He looks around. Though, again, there's no one out. Someone drives past in a pickup, but their windows are up and music is blasting.

"Because she's the one who ran the Blood Manor."

So that's why the name's so familiar.

"I didn't realize she was a collector," I say. "I thought she just built some wacky old house."

He nods. "She wasn't just building it for herself. Some say the antiques she collected compelled her to build. Like they were possessed or something."

Huh.

I'd never heard about that part. Then again, people are pretty tight-lipped about the Blood Manor.

"Come on," he says, continuing down the sidewalk. "I have to pee again."

I laugh, follow, and poke him in the side once, which makes him squeal and duck away and jog.

"Hey, wait up!" I say.

I follow him to his house, already discussing what

games we're going to play. But in the back of my mind, I'm wondering how to convince him to check out the ruins of the Blood Manor with me.

I have a feeling it's going to cost me a lot more than a few extra-large sodas.

2

Javier and I are floating on our backs in the pool, him in his atrocious tie-dyed board shorts and me in my usual pink T-shirt and trunks. He's got his phone streaming some trip-hop music station, and there's a floaty of cheese puffs and candy and more soda in between us. The sky has grown overcast, and heat lightning flickers farther off. Outside of the music, all I can hear are the cicadas buzzing in the endless cornfields surrounding his yard. We probably shouldn't be out here with the storm approaching, but neither of us moves to leave. We haven't said a word for at least twenty minutes. And I think that's one of the things I like most about our friendship—we've grown so close, we don't *have* to say anything to express ourselves.

Except I know I'm going to have to say something soon. If I don't, I'm going to explode.

Ever since leaving Mr. Hubbard's shop, all I can think about is going to the Blood Manor.

The place is outside Marshall Junction by a few miles, hidden in a tangled gnarl of trees and fields that no farmer claims as their own. I've ridden past it, like, a million times, and have even gone up to the fence separating it from the rest of the world. I've peeked in, just like everyone else. It was sort of a rite of passage when I hit middle school.

But I haven't gone inside. No one has.

And I know, with every fiber of my being, that I *have* to go if I ever want to find something worth finding.

"What are you scheming?" Javier asks.

I jolt and look over. Was I thinking aloud?

"What are you talking about?" I ask.

He grins and grabs a handful of cheese puffs and shoves them in his mouth, then washes his hand off in the pool. A cloud of orange cheese dust billows around him, and I remind myself not to jump back in. That orange is *impossible* to get out of pastels.

"You've got that look on your face," he says. That's it. Like I said, we know each other well.

I suppose there's no point delaying. *He* brought it up.

"I have a proposition for you," I say.

"Oh no."

I splash him with water.

"It's not that bad," I say. I try to keep my voice nonchalant as I say: "I want to explore the Blood Manor."

Javier laughs.

When I don't join in, he stops and says, "Wait, you aren't serious, are you?"

"Deadly serious," I reply.

"That's not a proposition," he says. "It's a death wish."

"You didn't let me finish!" I say. "Look, we both know we aren't going to find anything cool in Mr. Hubbard's antiques store anymore, and it's not like any of the estate sales we've been to have turned up anything."

"I dunno," he says, looking to the side of the pool. "I found a new friend."

I roll my eyes. He's staring at Ferdinand. The stuffed tutu-wearing mouse is currently on its own little lounge chair Javier stole from his sister's doll-house. There are even a few cheese puffs in a dish beside it.

"You're obsessed," I say.

"*You're* obsessed," he replies. He finally looks over to me. "Look, Kaden. You know I've got your back. You know I'm totally on board with treasure hunting and all that. But I'm not okay with breaking and entering and stealing. Even if the place wasn't *literally called the Blood Manor*, I'd be against it." He raises an eyebrow. "And I thought you would be, too."

"It's not stealing! Miss Hoffweller's been dead for decades, and she didn't have any heirs. No one has claimed the place. If anything, we'd be giving everything she collected a new life."

"Everything that didn't burn in a mysterious fire

that people say sounded like the screams of the dead," Javier interjects.

"Yes. That."

He sighs and grabs more cheese puffs.

"I just . . . Let me think about it," he says. "If we ever got caught . . ."

"We wouldn't."

He grumbles and stuffs a few more cheese puffs in his mouth.

I don't push it. Javier can be bullish when pressured, and the last thing I need is for him to turn on me. That's one of the biggest problems with having only one friend: When you fight, you don't have anyone else to turn to.

It's dark when I finally head home.

Javier offered to let me stay the night, but I knew I wouldn't be able to sleep. I couldn't stop thinking about the Manor, and what it would take to get him to go there.

Plus, he snores, so that's not happening.

It's only a twenty-minute bike ride, and most of that is through empty farmland, so it doesn't feel too scary wandering home in the dark. It's not like anything bad ever happens here. I've got my headphones in and my headlight illuminating the road in front of me. Fireflies dance through the cornfields, tiny sparks of yellow flickering as far as I can see. Which isn't really that far, since the corn is taller than I am.

When I get into town, I pedal a little faster. I'm okay being out in the middle of nowhere on my own. Corn doesn't try to hurt you. Fireflies don't harass you when they see you're alone.

I'm only a few blocks from my house when I turn the corner and see them.

Jake and Melvin and Gabby. The three people I very much did *not* want to see when I'm biking home alone late at night.

They're perched on Gabby's older brother's convertible—a junker that he fixed with spare parts—and staring at her phone. They're all in seventh grade with me, but they all seem so much *bigger*. Jake and Melvin are in wrestling and football, and Gabby goes hunting with her dad and is as mean as a bulldog. She scares me more than the others.

Which is why I freeze. Turn off my headlight. And very, very slowly start walking my bike backward, mentally calculating a safer route.

Gabby notices.

Of course she notices.

Her phone screen's glow goes dead, and without a word they slink off the car and prowl toward me, like feral cats. Or mangy dogs.

There's no use trying to flee. It's worse when I try to run. So I just roll my shoulders back and stand my ground and try to keep my breathing slow and steady even though it's trying to come out in short, rapid bursts. If they're the predators, I refuse to be the rabbit.

"Nice night," I say when they get closer. I don't know why, but speaking first feels like taking some control of the situation, even though I definitely don't have any. Not with them.

"Must be a full moon," Gabby says to Jake. "Freaks are out tonight."

Oh, she thinks she's witty, does she?

I bite my tongue.

"Freaks are always out," Jake says.

"Question is," Melvin says, "what are we gonna do about it?"

My blood turns to cold sludge in my veins. My breathing picks up its pace. *Don't be a rabbit, don't be a rabbit*. Even though, right then, all I want to do is run and hide.

"*Do?*" I ask. Okay, it's more of a squeak.

"Well, yeah," Gabby says. "We don't want any freaks in our town. Sets the wrong sort of press—press-a. What's the word?"

"Precedent?" I offer, then hate myself for it.

She glowers. "Yeah. Sets the wrong sort of precedent. Pretty soon everyone will be running around looking like . . ." She eyes me up and down. "Like *that*."

I can't help it: I glance down.

I'm in a loose sequin top and pastel blue shorts, old sandals. No makeup, no wild hair colors. Not after the pool. For me, this is pretty tame. And even then, even though I refuse to let these kids shame me for being different, I am still acutely aware that there are three of them, and although we are surrounded by houses, no one is looking out. I could scream, but then I'd get it worse later.

I am basically alone.

They step closer to me, crowding in.

Their closeness is more intimidating than bared fists, though the way they look at me tells me those aren't far behind.

"So, *freak*," Gabby growls. "You ready to be *taken care of*?"

She steps forward, only a few inches away.

And just then, the door across from us opens, and out steps Mr. Hubbard, holding a bag of trash.

"What are you kids doing out here?" he calls. "Kaden, is that you?"

Gabby and the others bolt before Mr. Hubbard can get a good look at them.

"Everything's fine, Mr. Hubbard," I call out.

Except it isn't fine. It isn't fine at all.

3

The next day dawns sticky and hot, just like every other summer day in this tiny town. Not a cloud in the blue sky, barely a breeze, which means when Javier texts asking if he can come over, all we do is sit in my bedroom and play video games.

I don't bring up the Blood Manor again.

I also don't mention my run-in with Gabby and her goons. Javier is a worrier, and if he learns she's been bullying me—again—he won't let me out of his sight. Which is endearing, but I don't want a bodyguard trailing me for the rest of our break.

"If you don't do something about this," Javier

says, gesturing to the shelves beside us while we wait for the next level to load, "people are going to start worrying you're a hoarder."

"By *people* you mean you, right?" I ask. "Because no one else comes in here. Except my parents, but they've given up on me."

I glance over to where he's looking, to the display that makes my parents sigh in defeat and shake their heads with woe, the reason my father never comes in here anymore to clean—though secretly I think he just uses it as an excuse to make me do it.

Illuminated glass shelves line two walls, extending from the floor to the ceiling and framing the window overlooking our backyard. Every inch of the shelves is taken up by my curiosities.

I have shelves of old jewelry, including a necklace in a glass case that my mom picked up in New York, and which was apparently on the *Titanic*. There are gemstones cut in different shapes, from skulls to owls to glittering obelisks. Stacks of coins from every continent. Rusted medical equipment that would (hopefully) never be used today. Worn playing cards with intricate hand-painted pips. A ventriloquist dummy missing its lower jaw. Two ceramic dolls whose eyes still open and close. The skeleton of a parrot in a thin glass dome. A mirror made of black obsidian. Ceramic cups with ravens rather than flowers painted on their rims.

And while the rest of my room is crowded with crumpled clothes and books and games, the shelves are pristine. Not a hint of dust on any gem, not a single smudge on the clear glass. Everything is perfectly in its place, arranged by color and age and size, so the walls are a rainbow of artifacts from every era. To my mom and dad—and apparently Javier—it's a mess. But to me, it's perfection.

"You're going to need a new shelf soon," Javier says. "You don't have any space left."

"Don't tempt me," I reply.

"Seriously, though. You're not planning on going to the Manor, are you?"

I jolt. The next level is ready onscreen and I focus on navigating the dungeon, rather than looking at him.

"What gave you that idea?" I ask.

"You had that look in your eye last night," he says. "And you've always been headstrong." He hesitates. "Just . . . don't go, okay? I've heard stories. My brother's friend broke in there once. He hasn't been the same since."

I don't respond. We've all heard the stories. Kids who return saying they see ghosts, that they hear Miss Hoffweller's voice in their closet. But those are just stories. Stories to give teenagers street cred, stories to keep the rest of us out.

"Promise," I say. I still don't look at him. Just blast another monster onscreen.

If I look at him, he'll know I'm lying.

We bike over to his house in the evening to swim in his pool again.

The sun is just setting above the trees when I make my way down the long, dusty gravel road back home.

I'm about halfway there when I hear a car coming toward me, and see the telltale cloud of dust approaching. I move to the side of the gravel road and come to a stop because people don't always drive on the right side once they get out into the country. They also rarely go the speed limit.

At least, I stop until I see who the car belongs to.

The convertible races toward me, and I know by now that they've seen me. Gabby's older brother, who's even meaner than she is, must be behind the wheel. But I have an idea of who's giving the directions.

I panic. Javier's house is a good half mile behind me, and they'd catch me before then.

I'm near a crossroads, and one way leads toward the forest. Toward the Blood Manor. I can lose them in there. Or at least hope they won't follow me toward the forbidden house.

It doesn't make rational sense but it feels like a better shot at survival—I take the side road and pedal hard into the woods.

As I pedal down the winding road, the crunch of gravel and roar of the engine behind me tells me that Gabby isn't giving up. Her brother honks the horn, and the noise nearly makes me fall off my bike. As the road narrows and winds down and down, the trees growing gnarled and tangled overhead, I realize my mistake. In the corn, I might have been able to hide or escape through the tall rows. Here, the undergrowth is filled with thorns and itchweed. I'm stuck on the road, with only one way to go: toward the Manor. And Gabby is close on my heels.

Despite the sweat and panic in my veins, I shudder as I bike deeper into the woods. There's a wrongness in the air, like oily ash that settles under my skin. It makes me want to turn around—not that I *can* turn around.

The dreadful sensation tells me I'm getting close.

Dead branches cross the road, and the gravel farther on is pockmarked with sinkholes and writhing with thick roots. I hop off my bike and toss it to the side—I can't bike past the debris, not without risking crashing. I just have to hope that Gabby gives up. There's no way her brother's junker of a car can get through here. Hopefully she won't follow on foot.

But even as I run down the debris-strewn road, I know that's a vain hope. I don't even need to hear the screech of the brakes or the slam of the car doors to know they are still following me. They've chased me this far; they won't give up now. The only thought ricocheting through my head is, *So much for not being the rabbit!*

The path becomes so overgrown I can't see the road anymore. Branches slash at my face, and brambles rip at my bare legs. I barely feel it through the rush of adrenaline and fear in my veins. Behind me, I hear Gabby and her friends following, snapping branches and cursing at the top of their lungs. I don't hear her brother; he must be waiting in the car.

"We're going to find you, Kaden!" Gabby calls out. "When we get you, you're dead! You can't hide from us!"

I run harder. I know she's telling the truth.

Then I crash into something that screeches like a banshee. A tree?

No.

A gate. A huge wrought-iron gate covered in vines. And through it, I see the sprawling ruins of an ancient house.

I've reached the Blood Manor.

4

The fire-marked house towers up in front of me, a desolate, mangled mess of blackened wood beams and rotting trees. It's less of a manor and more of a mausoleum. Between the vines on the gate, I can see toppled brick walls and charred remains of doorframes and fireplaces, half-crumbled gazebos and hedge mazes gone wild. In the bruised evening light, everything looks black and gray and violet.

At one point in time, the manor before me would have been massive, the largest building around. The ruins sprawl across the overgrown yard, the footprint easily bigger than a football field. The gardens and hedge mazes spread out to the side, along with out-buildings and ruined statues and staircases leading to nowhere. The remaining stone is pitted and pocked, as if diseased. Even after so many years, the forest hasn't really moved to reclaim the place. Or, if it had, it found that the Blood Manor didn't want to be reclaimed.

Despite the ruins and the fact that no one has been here, there isn't any new growth. No trees or new shrubs except for the hedges, not like the rest of the woods. No animals making nests in the twisted gutters. Nothing living. Nothing moving. It's like an old photo, worn and faded and suspended in time.

Everything looks wrong. Everything about it tells me to turn away.

But Gabby and her friends are closing in behind me. I can't turn away. The only way to escape them is to go in.

I glance behind me to see Gabby, Jake, and Melvin fighting their way through the undergrowth. Gabby catches sight of me and yells out in anger.

I find a space in the fence and duck inside.

It's not my imagination: The air drops twenty degrees the moment I'm past the fence. I shiver and fully expect to see my breath come out in clouds, but I don't turn back. I run forward, toward the safety of the house. There are dark shadows in there that can hide me. I hope.

The crunch of my feet on the gravel sounds like I'm running on snow. Or ice. Or bones. Didn't they say the place burned down in the winter? That the unearthly flames hadn't even melted the snow? The air is stagnant and smells like smoke and cinders, and it gets stronger as I near the giant house. As if the house were still burning. As if the flames were trapped in time like the rest of this place.

I reach a burnt-open door and duck inside.

In the gloom, I can just make out the grand reception hall. The timbers are burnt and a great staircase sweeps up in front of me, though it's cracked off at the top and looks like a skeletal jaw. I hesitate in the doorway. I don't want to go deeper. There's a sadness here that sinks into my bones, makes me want to drop to my knees and never move again, and that oil-slick wrong feeling is back and worse than ever.

Something crashes in the yard behind me. I look back to see Gabby, Jake, and Melvin catapulting themselves over toppled statues and slashing aside hedges. Even though I'm hidden in the shadows, Gabby's eyes pierce me to the spot.

"Just leave me alone," I whisper.

She doesn't. She won't. I have no choice but to run farther into the house.

I dart behind the staircase to a hall that stretches on into nothing. It's so dark I can't see my own feet, and I want to use my phone as a light. But I know that will draw Gabby to me. Waiting here in the dark for her to inevitably find me is also a bad plan.

Footsteps thud on the marble. She's inside, and when she calls my name, it sounds like she's only a dozen feet behind me. I creep forward slowly. I don't turn on my phone. I trail my hand along the wall and walk as carefully and quickly as I can. I try not to let my imagination get the better of me, try not to imagine my hand brushing over spiderwebs or touching slime or having my foot fall into an endless pit. Strangely, I don't touch anything besides the wall, which is cool and must be covered in ashen, old wallpaper. My feet don't knock into any debris or pits.

This place burned down. Surely there should be signs of that?

After another dozen steps, the hall turns, and I follow it to the right. It's only then, when I can't hear anything but my own frantic breathing, that I let myself pull out my phone and use the faint glow of the screen as a light.

The hall is completely empty.

There isn't any debris—no destroyed rafters or toppled furniture, only a film of ash on the black marble floor. The walls are lined with empty marble pedestals, everything blackened, with doors smudged black by soot dotted between. It's impossible to tell what the wallpaper once looked like. Now it's a black tunnel, something you'd find abandoned deep underground. Not even motes of dust float in the air. I feel completely alone—

Until I hear footsteps echoing behind me and the distant angry words of Gabby, Jake, and Melvin.

They haven't given up. Which only makes *me* want to give up. But if they catch me . . . if they catch me, I'll never be found again. Like Miss Hoffweller, I'll disappear in this empty mansion, become nothing more than another cautionary tale.

I'm not going to give up that easily.

A slightly open door beckons to my left. And it's not just another room: When I shine my light in, I see stone stairs going down. Unlike the other doors, this one had been bolted closed with a padlock in the past. The thick iron lock now hangs open from its hook. Chills race down my neck.

Whatever was down here must have been important to be locked away like that.

Every survival bone in my body tells me not to go down there, that I shouldn't be running headfirst into danger. But I keep envisioning what Gabby will do when she finds me, and before I can stop myself, I slip past the door and close it most of the way shut behind me. Maybe she won't notice the lock is open. Maybe she won't try to find me here.

But just in case, I'm not going to wait at the top of the steps.

I creep
        down
            the stairs,
                my footsteps
                swallowed up
                in the gloom.
                    Down
                    and
                    down
                    the steps go,
                spiraling slowly,
                until I realize I must be hundreds of feet
                below the surface.

Swathes of black sweep along the walls, like billows of flame had brushed along the sides with black wings. But there's no char on the ceiling or the steps. I trace one of the ashen lines down. My light lands on a door. A plain wooden door, shut tight.

Char marks spread out from its sides, definitely like two black fallen angel wings. There's no hint of soot on the door, though.

I creep forward hesitantly. There's no lock on this door. The crystal doorknob refracts my light into a burst of rainbows all over the walls, momentarily dazzling me.

It's only when I get closer that I realize the knob is shaped like a skull.

And when I put my hand on it, it is somehow warm.

The scent of burning fills my nostrils, but so, too, does a curious buzzing, an electricity I can't ignore.

I can't turn away.

I turn the knob and open the door.

The room inside is small, the size of my bedroom, with a low stone ceiling and walls covered in gaudy velvet fleur-de-lis wallpaper. At least, from what I can tell from the unburnt patches.

Metal lumps glitter among piles of ash. Some look like they might be gold, and gemstones peek out coyly from the soot. Nothing is intact along the walls. The fire consumed everything.

Everything, except . . .

I take a hesitant step forward.

There's a pillar in front of me. Made of simple stone.

Atop it is a small jewelry box of black lacquer.

It isn't burnt at all. It gleams in my light like it's been freshly polished.

And maybe it's my imagination, but it almost looks like the char is coming *from* that pedestal, long billows of soot burnt into the floor around it.

"What in the world?" I whisper.

I make my way toward it, trembling slightly, the bullies momentarily forgotten.

With shaking hands, I open the box.

The inside is pillowed in pink satin.

And resting right in the middle,

        absolutely pristine,

                is a ring.

A silver banded ring. But rather than a gemstone, the only embellishment is a hooded, gray glass eye. The kind of eye you'd see in an old doll.

Or perhaps even a human.

I swear it's staring

        right

        at

        me.

Warning bells scream in my head, but I don't heed them.

Something else compels me.

Whispers in my head.

Urging me forward.

I pick up the ring.

I slip it over my finger.

It fits perfectly.

From the empty shadows behind me, a voice screams out,

"THAT'S MINE!"

5

I scream and turn around, but I don't see anyone there, even though I *know* someone is there, can feel her presence in the room, can feel her eyes on the back of my neck. It isn't Gabby. The voice was a woman's. Old. And angrier than Gabby could ever be.

Shadows swirl around me. Congeal. My light flickers. It can't pierce through the darkness.

"Give it back!" the woman growls behind me.

And cold, dead fingers rake down my spine.

I run.

My light bobs like a firefly as I race up the stone steps, scrabbling over stone. I don't care if I'm running toward Gabby. I just know that she's less of a threat than whatever is chasing me.

I stumble when I reach the top step, skidding across the floor and crashing into a plinth. My phone cracks against the wall. The light goes out.

The hall goes pitch-black.

Behind me, the unseen woman screams in rage.

I race forward.

Through shadows that reach toward me.

Over stones that trip up my feet.

Past pedestals that crash at my heels.

The darkness ahead of me grows lighter, the same purplish bruise of the sky. I'm close to the exit. Just a little farther, just a little—

Shadows swirl before me. Twist and writhe and form a shape.

The shape of a woman.

She is horrifying.

Her gray hair billows around her like serpents. Her mottled skin is as white and translucent as rice paper. Her hands are clawed, with razor-sharp nails, and her elaborate black dress looks like layers of spiderwebs. But it's her face . . . her face that nearly stops me dead.

Her lips are cracked, peeled back over black gums and rotted teeth.

Her nose is severed, revealing the pits of her skull.

And her eyes are black depths, veined in purple.

She reaches toward me.

Screams with a howl that shatters the stained glass above us, sends shards cascading down.

And then she breaks apart in a billow of soot, to reveal Gabby, standing triumphantly in the arch of the doorframe.

"Well well well," she says. "Looks like *someone's* in trouble."

Gabby grabs me by the arm and drags me outside.

I can't stop screaming; I don't even know if I'm screaming at her or screaming because of the ghost.

I struggle against her.

I have to get away.

From her.

From here.

But her grip is strong. She tosses me on the ground and calls out to her friends, and it's only then, when my palms are bruised and the panic has turned to tears, that I'm able to speak.

"We have to get out of here," I warn. I struggle to stand but she kicks me down.

"Oh, you aren't going anywhere," she says.

I don't even feel her foot connecting to my shin. All I feel is panic, a buzz that won't break, and it has nothing to do with her or Jake or Melvin.

"You don't understand," I gasp as her friends near. "The house. It's haunted. There was a ghost."

Gabby howls with laughter, and so do her friends.

"Really?" she asks. "You expect me to believe that?"

She leans over, grabs me by the collar of my shirt. "The only ghost here is going to be you," she says.

She nods to Jake and Melvin, who crack their knuckles and step closer, chuckling menacingly.

Then, from the house, comes a scream.

My first reaction is to bolt, but even though Jake and Melvin look to the ruins uneasily, Gabby just laughs.

"Is that your boyfriend Javier?" she teases. "Sounds like the sort of scream he'd make."

I let the taunt slide off. I'm already backing away from the house. The ring burns like frostbite on my finger.

"He isn't here," I manage. "Like I said, it's a ghost—"

Gabby kicks me again. I cough and trail off.

"You think I'm stupid enough to fall for that? You're going to pay for that. Oh, you are going to *pay* . . ."

But Jake and Melvin aren't looking at me with the same malevolence in their eyes. They aren't looking at me at all.

They're still looking toward the Manor. I can't see what they're staring at—Gabby towers in front of me—but I can guess what they see.

"Gabby—" Jake begins.

"Not now," Gabby interjects. "I'm just getting started."

Melvin's eyes go wide. A strangled moan escapes his lips. Without another word, he runs off.

Gabby jerks her attention to him. "What are you—"

Another scream rips from the Manor. This time, it's accompanied by Jake, screaming at the top of his lungs before running after his friend.

Gabby finally turns around. When she does, she starts to stammer.

"W-w-what . . . what is *that*?" she manages.

I look past her. To see the horrible ghost woman floating in the doorway. Only, she isn't confined to the doorway. She's floating forward, toward us, and there is murder in her moon-white eyes.

"*Mine!*" the ghost woman screams out.

Gabby must finally realize this isn't a trick.

"What did you do?" she asks, staring at me briefly.

Without waiting for an answer, she takes off at a run, leaving me behind.

I cower there for only a moment. Just minutes ago, I was running away *from* Gabby. But the ghost woman is getting closer, and before she can reach me, I scramble to my feet and run *after* Gabby.

I barely notice the forest as I rush back up the long winding drive to the main road.

I don't look behind me.

I don't want to see if the ghost woman has followed.

Gabby is fast—faster than I am, at least—and she reaches the car before I'm even close to my bike. Melvin and Jake are already inside, and she leaps in the front passenger seat without pause, yelling at her brother to *go, go, go*. He guns the engine and reverses up the road, the tires squealing so loud none of them can hear me scream out to wait, to not leave me here.

They don't wait.

I stop, defeated, and watch them drive off.

It's only then that I look behind me.

The forest is empty.

No ghost.

No screams.

No eerie wrongness.

Just the woods and a darkening twilight.

I stand there, panting, staring through the undergrowth.

A twig snaps farther in.

Without waiting to see if it was a squirrel or the ghost, I hop on my bike and pedal for my life.

7

I cycle home in a daze. I don't catch sight of Gabby again. Though I'm not as worried about encountering her as I was before.

She was as scared as I was.

It's only when I reach the safety of my driveway that I finally stop moving, finally stop pedaling.

It's only there that I let myself pause and look behind me, down the long driveway, past the neighborhood and the fields and the forest, toward the ruins of the Manor, and ask myself the question I have no answer for:

Did that really happen?

Except, when I wonder that, I look down at my hand.

To the silver ring with its unblinking gray eye.

And I know, yes, it *did* happen.

Somehow.

Even though I don't truly understand what *it* is or was.

I leave my bike in the garage, sneak to my bathroom, and start the shower. I stare at myself in the mirror, still dazed, still not feeling like I'm really here.

I'm covered in dirt and dust and sweat and scrapes.

I look like a monster.

A monster with an eyeball on its finger.

I reach down to pull it off.

It won't budge.

"Must just be the dirt," I mutter. Or maybe my fingers swelled up from the heat and humidity. I've heard that can happen.

So I hop in the shower, still electric and buzzing from the narrow escape, my brain feebly trying to piece together the impossible events that just unfolded.

I was chased into the basement of the Blood Manor.

I found this ring.

And after . . . I have no clue what's been real and what's been my imagination. All I know is that I was chased out.

Was it a ghost that appeared? Was it Miss Hoffweller, demanding I return her ring?

That couldn't have been real. Ghosts don't exist.

And the more time I spend in my shower, lathering and trying to rinse clean the layers of muck and mystery, the less real it seems.

This is real: the salmon-pink walls and faded shower curtain, the bargain-bin shampoo and bodywash, the ragged Disney towel I've had since I was a little kid. Everything else . . . Maybe there was a gas leak or something in the Manor and I imagined things. Maybe I hit my head. Maybe the fear of being attacked by Gabby did something to my brain.

I don't know. All I know is that it couldn't have happened. At least, not the way I seem to remember it.

I get out of the shower, change into pajamas, and slip into bed.

When I get under the covers, I try one more time to take off the ring.

It still doesn't budge. It didn't even slide when I tried in the soapy shower.

"Whatever," I mutter. "Guess I'm stuck with you."

I reach over with my ringed hand to switch off my bedside lamp.

And right as the light clicks off—

right as the shadows shift—

I swear I see the ring blink.

8

I dream that I am buried.

I can't see.

Can't speak.

Can't breathe.

All I can do is stare out into the suffocating darkness. Unable to move. Unable to tell if time is passing or if I'm frozen.

Everything

is

darkness.

Until.

I hear it.

The shuffling of footsteps.

The creaking of timbers.

Someone

is

here.

I shudder at the thought. But I can't move to shiver. I am trapped.

Unless . . .

Light burns through the darkness.

A raging, purifying flame.

Like the raging, purifying flame that brought me here.

But no.

This is different.

Through the darkness I see something.

No. Some*one*.

They are clearly confused.

When I see the shadowed figure step closer, I am filled with hunger.

Hunger to move.

Hunger to seek.

Hunger to live again.

They reach out.

Light burns through me.

And when I can see, I realize the person standing over me is . . .

me?

9

"You don't look like yourself," Javier says. "Are you feeling okay?"

I'm over at Javier's playing video games like normal—there isn't much else to do in a town like this.

The truth is, when I woke up this morning, I *wasn't* feeling okay. Even though my AC was on full blast, I was covered in sweat. Burning up. But when I slipped into the bathroom to check my temp, I was at a perfectly normal 98.6. No fever. So why did I feel like I was melting? Why were there dark shadows under my eyes, like I hadn't slept a wink?

Was it the dream?

I'd woken up immediately after. It started to fade from my mind the moment I opened my eyes.

For some reason, it felt like I wasn't actually opening my eyes. It felt like I'd already opened them in the dream.

I don't tell him any of that. Javier already thinks I'm two steps away from losing it.

"Totally fine," I say. "Just tired. Was up late reading."

"Uh-huh," he mutters slowly, clearly not buying it. Or maybe he's just focused on the RPG.

I try to keep my face calm even though all I can think is, *He knows I went to the mansion.*

"I feel like you're hinting at something," I say.

"Well, yeah," he replies. He pauses the game. "New ring?"

Once more, the spike of adrenaline courses through me.

"Oh, this?" I ask, trying to play it cool. I prepared for this. Of course I did. If you stay prepared, you don't have to get prepared. "Nothing. Got it in the mail yesterday."

"Oh?" His eyebrow arches. He clearly doesn't

believe me. Then again, would I, if I were in his shoes? I'd mentioned the Manor before, and even though I hadn't *intended* to go, I'm not about to admit that Gabby chased me there. I don't want to tell him about any of that—about the ring, about the ghost, and definitely not about Gabby. He can be overprotective, but he's also no match for her and her friends. Which is why I came up with a cover story.

"Yeah. Found it online. Some boutique curiosity shop in Hollywood. They had loads of cool stuff, but this was about all I could afford from my allowance." I grin. "They had some rogue taxidermy, too, if you wanted to get Ferdinand a friend."

Rogue taxidermy is when the artist takes different animals (ethically sourced! Usually it's, like, roadkill) and combines them to create mythic creatures, like chupacabras or chimeras or jackalopes. Or sometimes they just take a normal animal and make it pose unnaturally, like Javier's ballerina mouse.

I reach for my phone to show him the website—I *did* research to find an oddities shop in Hollywood, and it *did* sell rings with glass eyes attached. Just not ones found in haunted mansions.

Probably.

Never know with Hollywood.

He takes the phone.

"I think Mom would kill me if I bought any more taxidermy," Javier mutters, scrolling through the site. "But what do you think, Ferdinand? Would you like a bat friend?"

He holds the phone up to the stuffed mouse, showing it a bat with four wings.

"Sometimes I worry about you," I mutter.

He hands the phone back. "I'm not the one wearing someone's old eye on their finger. Which . . . can I see it?"

I hold out my hand. He takes it, and I try not to grimace—he's been eating cheese puffs again, and his fingers are that gross powdery-sticky combination.

"It looks so realistic. Do you think it's from a body?"

I shudder. "I hope not," I say.

He pulls my hand closer, peering intently.

"Whoa, you can almost see the veins in the eye . . ."

At that moment, his finger brushes the ring.

It feels like lightning burning through me.

My eyes roll in the back of my head and my vision goes white. I feel my body contort and constrict, feel myself rising up on my toes while a horrible voice roars inside me:

MINE!

"Jeez, okay," I distantly hear.

And in a flash, it's over.

I'm sitting on the bed and Javier has dropped my hand. He's looking at me like *he's* the one who is hurt.

"No need to get all aggro about it," he says.

Wait.

That angry voice in my head . . . had that been me? Did I say that out loud?

"Sorry," I say. But even as I say it, a very different emotion floods through me: I don't feel sorry for growling at him. Instead, I'm filled with rage that he tried to touch my ring without permission.

That he tried to take it from me.

I push the emotion down, and it, too, fades, just like the pain that already seems like a distant memory.

Why would I care if he touched the ring? Why

would I even care if he wanted to borrow it?

"Don't worry about it," he says. "But for the record, I wasn't going to take it. Way too creepy for me."

"Yeah," I say. "Of course."

Because I don't know what else to say.

I don't know where that rage came from.

I just know that it wasn't mine.

10

Despite my strange outburst, I hang at Javier's for the rest of the afternoon. It's the last day of summer break, and it's in the triple digits outside, so we spend most of it playing video games in the air-conditioning. We don't bring up the ring or what happened again.

Stranger still, I can't really find it in me to think about it.

I mean, I *know* I should be freaked out. At least a little. I've washed my hands a few times but no matter how soapy and cold I get my fingers, the ring refuses to budge. Not to mention I'm positive I saw a ghost last night, which should absolutely send me into a panic. Except . . .

Every time I think about it, it's like someone turns my head the other way. One moment I am on the edge of a panic attack, and the next, I can't figure out what I was worried about in the first place. When I worry about not taking off the ring, all I can think is, *Why would you want to take it off, anyway?* When I wonder what came over me when Javier touched the ring, my gut tells me that it was all perfectly normal. And the ghost? The moment I think about *her*, my brain tells me I was just hallucinating: It was just stress, brought on by being chased by Gabby and fearing for my life.

Which makes me wonder . . . is Gabby freaking out about this, too? It's the one thought that doesn't shift away: I wonder how she's doing. And that's not a thought I've ever had before.

After a dinner of pizza and doughnuts, we decide to lounge in his pool for one last hurrah before tomorrow.

Javier heads into the kitchen to grab some more snacks, and I make my way out to the back door. As I walk down the hall, passing framed photos of him and his family, something catches my eye in a hanging mirror.

A shadow in the corner of the mirror.

A face that isn't mine.

I freeze.

So, too, does the ring on my hand.

It's not the face of the ghostly Miss Hoffweller. No, this is the shadowy face of a young boy, his clothes from another century.

And he has only one eye.

One

gray

eye.

But unlike the ghost of Miss Hoffweller, this specter doesn't lunge at me. It doesn't scream out.

It just smiles at me. A smile that makes my blood go cold.

Oh yes, I swear I hear him say. *You'll do quite nicely.*

He reaches toward me—

and a hand clamps down on my shoulder.

I scream and turn around.

It's just Javier.

My heart thuds a million beats a minute and my

breath races. I look back to the mirror. But it reflects only Javier and me. I look as terrified as I feel, and Javier looks confused.

"I was going to ask if you were admiring yourself," he says. "But a scream sort of negates that."

"I . . ." My hand is clutched to my chest. I keep looking down the hall and back to the mirror. But the shadowy boy never appears. I don't know if that's a good or a bad thing.

I decide to tell Javier, "It's nothing."

He raises an eyebrow. "Maybe you should lay off the sugar for the rest of the night. I've never seen you this jumpy."

And right then, I change my mind and want to tell him everything. I want to tell him about Gabby chasing me to the Manor, about finding the ring in the depths and being chased out by a ghost. I open my mouth. But the moment I try to speak, the ring freezes against my skin, so cold and sharp all that comes out of my lips is a gasp.

"Are you sure you're okay?" he asks.

I clutch my hand. The ring instantly goes back to its normal temp, and the pain fades to memory.

What is happening to me? I want to ask.

But I'm afraid the words won't come out.

"It's nothing," I find myself saying instead. "You just scared me."

His eyebrow rises even higher.

"Right," he says. He clearly doesn't buy it. But thankfully, he doesn't keep questioning me. "Well, come on. My parents want you out before it gets too late. Apparently, I have to get on a normal sleep schedule."

I nod and follow him to the pool.

By the time I'm out there, whatever fear I'd had from seeing the ghostly figure in the mirror has vanished.

And when I leave his house, so, too, is the memory of what I saw there.

II

That night, I dream I am in a manor.

The house is bigger and grander than anything I've ever seen.

A great staircase sweeps up to the second floor, and ornate tapestries and paintings from every corner of the globe hang on the ornately wallpapered walls. Artifacts stand regally atop marble pedestals—statues of robed, ghostly women from Greece, pottery depicting the underworld from ancient Egypt, grotesque papier-mâché beaked masks from Italy. Every one of them is unique and important, and my fingers itch to collect them.

They would work so well in my oddity collection.

As I wander past the stairs, I realize I've been here before. Which means this manor is *in* Marshall Junction. What are all these priceless artifacts doing here?

Things click slowly.

I'm in the Blood Manor . . . *before* it burned down. And I know, without a shred of doubt, that this isn't just a dream. I walk over to one of the statues and run a hand over it. The granite is smooth and cold under my fingers. The air smells faintly of firewood. I am here. Really here.

Somehow, I know, this is real.

The thought scares me. Shouldn't I be waking up? Whenever I've realized I was dreaming before, I've woken up immediately. But this dream doesn't stop. If anything, it gets stronger, more solid.

Especially because, down the hallway, I hear crying.

Curiosity hooks in my chest and pulls me forward. I make my way toward the noise, my feet silenced by the plush throw rugs. All I hear is the crying. Louder with every footstep.

It sounds like more than one person.

More than one kid.

I realize, too, that this is the hallway I walked down only yesterday.

This is where I found the ring.

When I get closer to the sound of the crying, I understand that the sounds of despair are coming from behind that very door.

I reach out for the handle.

"What are you doing here?" comes a woman's voice behind me. "You shouldn't be here."

I turn to see an older woman in a long green dress standing in the hallway. Her hair is grayed and long, cascading around her shoulders and over the many chunky gold necklaces she wears. Her wrists are adorned with beautiful bracelets, and her clasped hands drip with rings. I know, in that moment, that this is the famed Miss Hoffweller.

"It's dangerous for you to be here," she says. Her hazel eyes are wide. "You shouldn't—"

Her gaze has snared on my hand. On my ring.

"How did you get that?" she whispers.

"I found it," I say. I take a step backward and

brush against the door locking away the crying children. "Here."

I expect her to rush at me. To scream. To demand that I give the ring back, like her ghost had earlier.

Instead, she starts to cry.

"You poor, poor dear," she says. She rubs her hands together worriedly, and it's then that I notice one finger is bare. I know, somehow, that she once wore the gray-eye ring on that finger. "He has you now."

I swallow. Fear rises in my chest, and the crying behind me doesn't help. Especially because one of the kids has started to scream.

"Who . . ." I can barely get the question out, I'm so scared of the answer. "Who has me?"

She shakes her head sadly.

"It's too late," she replies. Tears fall harder. "It's best not to fight. Do as he asks. Otherwise . . ."

Behind me, every kid locked in the cellar starts to scream out. Miss Hoffweller looks past me.

"He comes," she whispers.

And then, like a billow of smoke, she vanishes.

Floorboards creak behind me.

I turn slowly. The ring burns white-hot on my

finger, clamps so tight I scream out, fearing it will slice my finger clean off.

Pain turns my vision white.

In the blinding pain, I hear a boy's high, sinister laugh.

The ring throbs on my finger. I try to take it off. But I know it's too late.

Wake up. Wake up. Please wake up!

As the kids in the cellar scream for help, a hand grabs my own, the grip rough and calloused.

"There is work to be done," a boy demands. "It's time to wake."

My vision clears.

But it isn't my vision.

I stare through a heavy-lidded circle.

I stare up.

At myself. No. At a pale boy with a malevolent grin. Only he is me . . . And then I realize . . .

I realize I am staring up through the ring.

12

It's already sweltering when I shuffle toward school the next morning.

Since Javier lives farther away, I wait for him out front and stare out at the crowd of gathering kids. They talk and laugh and share stories about summer break. It's a small school—only a few hundred kids— and it's not like they haven't been hanging out all summer together, anyway. But the first day back always feels momentous in a way. A change.

No one comes up to talk to me or ask how my summer's been. So I sit and play a game on my phone, waiting for Javier to show.

When a shadow falls over me, I figure it's him.

"We need to talk," the visitor says.

I look up with a jolt and nearly drop my already cracked phone.

Gabby.

She stands there with her arms crossed over her chest, and she looks at me with the same hatred she's always had. But the fire in her eyes isn't burning so bright. In fact, when we make eye contact, she looks away.

I don't say anything. Two nights ago she nearly beat me up, and now she wants to talk?

"Have you . . . have you been sleeping okay?" she asks, still not looking at me.

Definitely not the question I was expecting. "What?" I gasp.

She quickly glares at me, then looks back to the crowd of other kids. It's clear she doesn't want to be talking to me and definitely doesn't want to be *seen* talking to me.

"Don't act stupid," she says. "After we went to the Manor . . . Have you had any strange dreams?"

"No," I lie, because I'm not going to show any

more weakness around her. I don't want to give her any more ammunition. "Why?"

"Nothing," she says abruptly, and walks away.

I watch her go back to Jake and Melvin. Less than a minute later, Javier sits down next to me.

"Sooo," he says. "What was that all about?"

"No idea," I reply. Why was she asking about dreams?

"I'm surprised she actually talked to you," he mutters. He hands me his soda, and I take a sip. It's orange flavored, so it counts as breakfast. "I don't think I've seen her say a word to you since kindergarten."

We used to be friends, Gabby and me. I still don't know why she started hating me. Maybe I'd stolen one of her toys at the park or something. It's not like I've ever had the chance to ask—it's hard to want to talk to someone when their usual response is pushing you away or beating you up.

I shrug.

It feels like another lie, not telling him about what happened at the Manor. But I can't. And not just because I'm afraid the ring will stop me from saying it. He's my only friend—if he thinks I'm losing it, he'll stop talking to me, too. He may have an active imagination, but I doubt even he would believe me if I told him I was seeing ghosts. Especially since that would mean admitting I lied to him earlier.

The bell rings, and we make our way inside before I can start feeling too guilty.

Right before the door closes behind us, a shudder goes down my spine. Even though it's like a million degrees inside the school, I break into chills.

Someone is watching me.

I turn around.

There, across the street, is the shadowy boy I saw in my dream. I nearly stumble into Javier.

The boy is smiling. I can't see his eyes—his *eye*—but I can feel his gaze on me.

Then a bus drives past.

When it's gone, so, too, is the ghost.

13

I feel like I'm being watched for the rest of the day.

I keep glancing out the window in class, fully expecting to see the shadowed boy standing outside. The sensation is so strong that I opt to sit as far from the windows as possible, even though they're the only source of airflow and the classrooms feel like ovens. Even Javier notices my twitchiness—he catches me looking out the window and mouths, *Are you okay?*

I shrug.

The shadowy figure never shows again, but that doesn't mean he isn't there.

To make matters worse, the ring doesn't stop itching.

It feels like there's an electric current running through it, a prickling that almost-but-not-quite hurts. Every time I consider pulling it off, however, the sensation changes, becomes a cooling, calm wave. Comforting.

I don't take it off.

Why would I?

"Okay, what's going on?" Javier asks at lunch.

We sit at our usual table, away from everyone else, but I still glance around like he yelled it to the whole cafeteria.

"What are you talking about?"

"That!" he says. "What you just did. You're super jumpy. Did Gabby threaten you this morning or something?"

"I, she . . . no."

"Then what is it?" He actually looks a little hurt. "You've been acting strange ever since you got that ring."

Instantly, I clamp my free hand over it, hiding it from his view.

"I have not," I say.

His eyes narrow. "You just did it again."

I sigh and slouch.

And I'm about to tell him. I swear I'm about to tell him everything—getting chased to the Manor, finding the ring, seeing the ghost, and even the strange dreams and visions.

I open my mouth—

and the ring burns cold on my fingers

and behind Javier, a few tables away, I see the ghost boy.

The ghost boy glowers at me.

He shakes his head and points to Javier.

Then he slices a finger across his neck. I know the threat: If I tell Javier anything, Javier will be in trouble.

"It's nothing," I say instead of the truth. "Just tired. First-day nerves."

The moment the words leave my lips, the ghostly figure vanishes.

Javier sighs.

"You know you can tell me the truth," Javier says. "I would have hoped, by now, you knew that."

"I do," I say. "Promise."

I just can't tell you this. For your own sake. But I wish I could.

14

I know I should be freaking out.

I'm being followed by a ghost. A ghost that just threatened my best friend. But just like when I was thinking about the Blood Manor, I can't find the panic. Sure, I keep glancing over my shoulder. I'm jittery with anxiety, and I know I'm being followed. Watched. But the fear doesn't stick. Every time my heart starts to race, every time my brain tries to scream out that *this isn't normal*, the ring radiates that calming cold, and the anxiety and fear fall away. When I try to worry about my lack of worry—well, the same thing happens.

I know something is wrong.

My body just won't let me get worked up about it.

The one thing that *does* make me the kind of nervous that sticks is Gabby and her friends. I catch sight of them watching me throughout the day. Gabby has that same worried expression, but Melvin and Jake—Jake especially—are glaring at me, full stop.

I try to ignore it.

But during gym, when we're running laps, Jake makes it impossible to ignore.

"What did you do to us?" he growls when he nears me.

I look over at him, bewildered—how is he not panting? We're on the fourth lap, and I feel like I'm about to melt into a puddle of goo. Javier already gave up a lap ago and is walking the whole thing, meaning he's on the other side of the sweltering gym.

"What are you talking about?" I huff. I slow my pace, hoping Jake will run faster, but he stays right at my side.

"You know what I'm talking about. You did something in the Manor. I know it!" His outburst makes a few kids look at us, but most ignore him. I'm not the only one Jake picks on, and besides, I think most kids are just focused on not passing out, like I am. Like I *was*.

"I don't—"

"I've been there dozens of times," he says. "I've never seen . . ." He shakes his head. So much for the rumor that no one ever ventured there. Then his eyes alight on my ring, and a strange mix of triumph and fear crosses his face. "You weren't wearing that when you went in. But you had it when you came out. Did you steal it?"

"I—"

"It's all your fault," he says. He's nodding to himself like it's all adding up. "You did this. You did this to us."

"I didn't—what are you even talking about?"

Jake's eyes are wild now.

"You've seen him, haven't you?" Jake asks. "The ghost. He's been following me since we left the Manor. Gabby and Melvin, too. It's because of you. You let him out. You, and that ring!"

Before I realize what he's trying to do, he grabs for my hand.

His fingers touch the ring.

My vision explodes.

Images flash, flickering in bursts of light and shadow.

A long hallway, lit by lamps and thick with shadows.

A wooden door ahead.

A young girl crying at my side.

"Don't cry, don't cry," I say.

The girl looks up at me.

"I want my Mommy, Miss Hoffweller."

"She's down here," I reply.

We walk closer. Children cry behind the door.

My grip tightens on her hand. The gray-eye ring stares up at me.

It purrs with victory. With hunger.

He is always hungry.

"I don't want to go down there," she says.

"It's okay," I reply. "It will all be over soon."

I reach into my pocket for the key. Inside, I scream. I fight. *This is wrong!*

But on the outside, I am calm. My hand doesn't shake as I pull out the key.

As I unlock the padlocked door.

"Downstairs, sweet one," I say. "Then we will find your mommy."

The girl sobs. She does as she's told.

They all do as they're told.

When she takes a few steps down the stairs, I lock the door behind her.

I hear her pound against the door. But I ignore her cries.

I look into the hall mirror.

Two reflections stare back.

A boy, smiling. Shadowy. An overlay. A shade.

And a woman. Janice Hoffweller.

In the mirror, Janice screams silently.

At least, until the boy regains control of her.

Then, she smiles.

I stumble and fall to my hands and knees. Jake staggers to the ground beside me. He catches himself before falling, stumbling and taking a few steps away.

"What . . . what was that?" he stammers.

"I don't know," I reply. Fear races through my veins. *Did he see that, too?*

I push myself up to standing as other kids run

around us and the coach starts to come over, making sure we're okay. Am I okay? *What is going on?*

"Stay away," Jake warns. "Just stay away from me. You freak!"

He jogs off, leaving me standing there, too shocked to move.

"Do you need to sit out?" the coach asks.

I nod silently and let him lead me over to the bleachers.

I'm numb as I sit there, watching the class run. Javier gives me a *what's going on?* look, but I turn away. I don't know what's going on. It feels like I'm losing my mind, and no matter how numb the ring makes me to it, it still weirds me out.

Something is very, very wrong with me.

My gaze snares on Jake, who's finishing up his laps. A horrible voice growls in the back of my head. The voice from the visions. The voice from the dreams.

The ghost that has been following me.

It's time to begin again, he says.

Despite myself, I begin to laugh.

15

"Are you feeling okay, honey?" Mom asks at dinner.

Frustration grows inside me. Everyone keeps asking me that. And no, I'm not okay. But also, I'm totally fine. Why does everyone keep asking?

"I'm fine," I say, trying not to growl.

"Are you sure?" Dad asks. "You haven't touched your dinner. We made your favorite."

His prodding makes me want to scream. I keep my face as passive as I can.

In the back of my mind, all I can hear is the ghost's voice, telling me it's time to begin, time to begin. Whenever I blink, all I see is Jake's face. And that's not a face I want to see when I close my eyes.

I don't know what it means. All I know is I want to tell my parents to leave me alone.

All I know is that the ring burns and buzzes against my finger, fills my veins with fire, with anger.

That anger has filled me ever since gym. So much that I avoided Javier. I couldn't stand his questions, his concerned looks.

"Actually," I say now to my parents, "you're right. I'm not feeling well. I think I'm gonna try to go to bed."

I don't need to look at their faces to know they look at each other with concern. I can feel it.

Just as I don't have to look at my untouched plate to know that I don't want to eat. They say it's my favorite, and in some corner of my mind I know it should be, but it all looks disgusting. I'm hungry for something else.

I also know that if I stay here much longer, I'm going to say something I'll regret later.

My parents mumble some sort of acknowledgment, but I'm already up and heading toward my room.

When I get there, sleep is the last thing on my mind.

The buzz of the ring has grown to a roar in my head, a surge that's settled under my skin. An electricity that threatens to tear me apart.

I pace back and forth in my room, trying not to make too much noise but unable to keep still.

I keep glancing at the artifacts lovingly arranged on their glass shelves.

I keep wondering why I collected them in the first place.

They're junk. Each and every one of them.

I want to throw them all away.

I pause in front of an antique mirror. Feel my vision waver as I look into the warped glass.

I see my reflection staring back.

I see the face of a young kid.

I see the face of the one-eyed boy.

I don't know which is mine.

"It's time to begin again," I say to myself. My reflections smile.

16

I dream I'm walking. Walking through my hometown.
It is late. Deep night. My town feels abandoned.

It's sticky and hot in the dream, but the sensation
is far removed. As is the feeling of the cracked concrete underneath my bare feet. I stalk down the
empty street, my fists clenched and resolve burning
in my chest.

It's time to begin. It's time to begin.

In the dream, I am walking through a nearby
neighborhood. I pass a fence with a dog sleeping
out front. In the real world, the Doberman would
have leaped and growled at me. But in the dream, it

cowers as I pass, whimpering and running away.

Blink.

And I am in front of a house. Single story. Ranch rambler. White siding, picket fence, flickering porch light.

I've seen it before—I know every part of Marshall Junction—but I don't know who lives here.

I know who lives here.

I stay to the shadows. I walk around the back.

I pause outside the window.

I look inside. And smile.

Blink.

I shuffle away. Back through the shadows.

It is harder now, with this weight atop me. Harder, but not impossible.

In the dream, I am strong. Much stronger than when I'm awake.

Much faster, too.

Trees scratch up around me, the slivered moon casting bare light on the tangled ground. It shouldn't be enough to see, but I see everything in the sharpest of details. The bats sweeping between branches. Crickets scurrying beneath leaves.

My prize, fluttering his eyelids.

"Hush, now," I whisper. "Sleep. We are nearly there."

He groans, but my influence is strong. He slumbers.

Blink.

We are there.

The Manor rises before me. The blackened remains scratching at the sky.

I bring him inside.

Down the blackened hallway.

Toward the cellar door.

He stirs.

"What . . . what are you . . . ?" he grumbles.

I drop him from my shoulders.

On the concrete floor.

In the blackened cellar.

"Wait here," I tell him. "Be a good boy and wait."

"Who . . . ?" he asks. Sleep overtakes him once more.

I lean him against the wall.

When I leave and lock the door behind me, I begin to whistle.

This will be easier than I thought.

17

"Did you hear?" Javier asks at lunch the next day.

I'm not nearly as grumpy as I was yesterday, and he took my apology in stride. Not the first time I've been moody, and probably not the last.

"Hear what?" I reply.

He looks around conspiratorially, even though there is no one within hearing distance.

"Jake is missing," he says.

I shrug. I've never cared about Jake. Why would I start now?

I shovel another spoonful of mashed potatoes into my mouth. Even though I had a huge breakfast this morning, I am *starving*. Probably because I didn't eat anything for dinner.

"So?" I ask between mouthfuls.

"So?" he asks. "That's it? Don't you think it's sort of strange?"

"Not really," I reply. "He's a jerk. He probably did something really bad and is hiding because he doesn't want to face the consequences."

"But saying goodnight to your parents and then disappearing in the middle of the night?" he asks. "No note, no nothing."

"Was there a sign of struggle?" I ask.

"What? No. Why would you ask that?"

"Because then it means he left by his own free will," I say. "Come on, you know how much I love crime documentaries. If there's no sign of struggle, or breaking and entering, he probably just left in the middle of the night. Probably to do something illegal. Guarantee you he's back by the weekend."

Javier hesitates, then asks, "What did Jake talk to you about yesterday?"

"What?"

"During gym. He said something to you. It looked like you got into a fight."

"You think I had something to do with his disappearance," I say. Because, yeah, I've seen a lot of crime shows. If I was the last person to speak to Jake—especially to have an argument—then I'm the number one suspect.

Great.

Frustration grows inside me: It's not like I *wanted* to be on Jake's radar. Or Gabby's. Or Melvin's.

I want them all to leave me alone.

I want Javier to leave me alone, too.

"What?" Javier says. "No, I don't think you made him disappear. I mean, no offense, but I'm pretty certain Jake wouldn't have any issue defending himself against you."

The anger in me bubbles. The ring burns ice-hot on my finger.

"Oh? So you think I'm weak? I can't defend myself?"

Javier's mouth widens in shock.

"Kaden, that's not it at all. What in the world has gotten into you? I thought we just made peace."

But I barely hear his words.

Blood pumps so loudly in my ears that I can't hear anything at all, and beyond Javier's shoulder I can see the shadowy ghost, can feel his smile even though I can't see his face, and the anger burns against my fear.

"Are you okay?" Javier asks for the millionth time.

He reaches out for my shoulder.

"Don't touch me!" I yell out.

I leap from the seat and crash into a kid walking behind me.

"Hey!" the kid yells. I shove him back in response. He falls into another kid, and the whole cafeteria goes silent.

The shadowy figure is gone, but I know he's still there. I can feel him. Can feel his anger, his rage. Can feel it becoming my own.

"Kaden—" Javier says softly. "Come on, just sit down."

But I can't sit down. The anger burns and everyone is staring.

Before he can say anything else, before one of

the teachers can come over and ask me what's wrong for the millionth time, I turn from the table and run.

No one tries to stop me, not even Javier, and that makes me even angrier.

I run down the hall, but I don't leave the school. Instead, I yank open the door to a bathroom and shut myself inside.

Once there, I go to the sink and turn on the water and scrub my hands.

The water gets hot fast, but I don't turn it down. The scalding pain feels good. It burns away the heat of my anger, the bite of my fear, the cold of the ring.

I splash the hot water on my face, trying to jolt myself out of it, trying to come back to myself. Every movement aches. When I woke up this morning, I was sore all over. My shoulders ached, my calves were tight, and even though I told myself it was because of gym, I know the truth.

As much as I try to fight it, I remember the dream. Only now, I don't think it was a dream after all.

I remember going to Jake's house. I remember bringing him back to the Manor with impossible strength.

I remember locking him in the basement.

Just like all those other kids had been locked away years ago.

I'm becoming just like Miss Hoffweller.

I'm becoming a monster.

"I'm sorry," I whisper to Jake. Tears roll down my face. I don't know if they're from frustration or pain or fear. "I didn't mean it. I didn't mean for any of this to happen."

"Didn't mean for any of *what* to happen?" comes a voice behind me.

I jolt and look around.

Javier's followed me.

18

"Kaden," Javier says slowly, gently, like he's trying to calm a cornered dog. "What is going on? Come on, you can tell me. This isn't like you at all."

I open my mouth to speak, but right as I'm about to, I see a shape behind Javier. The ghost of the one-eyed boy. He shakes his head slowly, gesturing again with his finger that if I speak, Javier will be killed.

"I can't," I gasp.

"Kaden . . ."

"You don't understand," I say. "He's watching me. He knows."

Javier looks over his shoulder. The ghost vanishes in that motion, but I know that even if it was still there, Javier wouldn't see it.

"Who? Kaden, no one is here."

I try to speak.

Nothing comes out.

Javier watches me for a little longer. Then he sighs.

"I'm worried about you," he says. "You've been acting so strange lately. Growing distant. It isn't like you. Not at all."

My body shakes. In an instant, it feels like someone has poured cold water over my skin. Every muscle in my body tightens, just for a moment. And when my muscles relax, it feels like I'm back in a dream. Like I'm watching this all through someone else's eyes. Everything feels distanced. Removed.

"Well, maybe you don't know me that well," I state. My voice is strange. It doesn't sound like me. It's too gravelly, too gruff. The words leave my mouth before I can stop them.

They aren't what I want to say at all.

It's clear my words hit home. Javier winces and takes a step back, clearly hurt.

"What—"

"I didn't ask you to come in here," I continue. "I don't want your help. Or your concern."

"Kaden—"

"Don't you get it?" I ask. "I don't want you around, weirdo. Get. Out!"

Javier takes another step back. There's a pain in his eyes I've never seen before.

In my head, I scream out my apologies. I can't open my mouth, can't move my arms.

I am trapped in my own body, and I can't do a thing to change it. Instead, I stand there, glaring at him, my fists clenched.

"If that's how it is," he finally says.

He turns and leaves, letting the door close behind him.

A few seconds pass.

And then, I turn around.

To face the grubby mirror.

To see my face, and the shadow's face, and for

a horrifying moment I once again can't tell which is actually mine.

"You will tell no one," I whisper in that same gravelly growl. I smile. "You are mine. And there is much work to be done."

19

When I leave the bathroom, it feels like everyone in the school is watching me.

In every class.

In every hallway.

I feel their eyes.

I thought I had learned to deal with the curious stares, the angry glares. But this is different. This is new.

As I walk down the hall, people aren't just looking at me to make me uncomfortable.

They're looking at me because *I'm* making *them* uncomfortable.

Kids whisper as I pass or stare over their shoulders when the teacher isn't looking. The only person who isn't watching me is Javier. He avoids me in class, sitting as far away as possible. He looks the other way when we pass in the halls. Just like yesterday, I've pushed him away.

This time, I don't think I can pull him back.

This time, I don't *want* to pull him back.

When the day is finally over, I stand at my locker grabbing my books. Everything feels like it's in a haze, like I'm still sleepwalking. I put books in my bag without even looking at their spines. Grab notebooks and folders without seeing if they're for the right subjects.

The sensation of being overpowered, of being controlled, has faded away. It left me feeling hollowed out and empty.

In a strange way, I almost miss the sensation. Because even though I couldn't move, even though I couldn't control myself, in those few moments with Javier, I felt *powerful*.

I pause, reaching for a book, and stare at the ring.

This time, I know it's not a trick of the light.

The eye *moves*.

I gasp, and before I can try to yank the ring off, someone shoves me and flips me around, slamming me against the locker.

Gabby.

"What did you do to him?" she demands.

A few kids walk past, but no one stops, and there isn't a teacher nearby to help. It's just me, and her and Melvin glaring at me.

"Wh-who?"

"Don't play stupid," she says. "We know you did something to him!"

The trouble is, I'm bad at lying. I know precisely who she's talking about, and I also know I'm guilty. I just don't know how, or why.

"I know he confronted you yesterday," Melvin said. "What did you say? What did you do?"

"Nothing!" I manage.

"Stop lying!" Gabby yells. She slams her fist into the locker, right by my head. I flinch. "I know you did this to us. I know this is your fault. Something happened when you went into the Manor. That's the only explanation. We've been there a thousand times before and we've never been . . ." She trails off. Clearly, she can't bring herself to admit out loud that she was being haunted.

"Gabby, look," Melvin says. "Kaden's ring . . ."

Gabby stares at my hand.

"Where did you get that?" she asks.

"I—" I begin.

"I bet you stole it," Melvin says to me. His voice rises in fear. "That's what's causing all of this. This is one of Miss Hoffweller's old things. She's probably trying to get it back!"

He grabs my hand, and two terrible things happen at once.

The ring goes ice-cold. That horrible calmness washes over me, takes over me.

And the ring's eye *moves*. Looks straight at Melvin. With unnatural speed and strength, I grab Melvin's wrist with my other hand. I feel his wrist crunch and grind beneath my fingers.

"Don't you ever touch me again," I snarl. My voice isn't quite my own.

Melvin tries to struggle free, but my grip is strong. His arm doesn't move an inch.

"Ow! Kaden! You're *hurting me*."

"Let him go, Kaden," Gabby warns.

I don't move. I just stare at Melvin. Squeeze his wrist tighter until he cries out in pain. The eyeball ring watches his face contort.

Then Gabby shoves me.

I slam into the locker, releasing Melvin's hand as the horrible calmness releases me. I slump against the cool metal, panting. I clutch my ring, just as Melvin clutches his injured wrist.

I can see the purple and red bruising on his skin.

Did I . . . did I do that?

"What happened?" I whisper. I remember Gabby approaching me. I remember Melvin taking my hand. And then . . . this.

Melvin scrambles back away from me. Gabby supports him.

"Come on," she says to him. "Let's get you out of here."

I watch them go.

And as they leave, I hear a voice whisper by my ear. The one-eyed boy's voice.

"He's next."

20

The rest of the night is a blur.

I know I get home and make small talk with my mom and dad.

I know we have dinner. I make an effort to eat . . . but only so they won't ask me about it.

I know I do my homework.

I know, because at one point I look up and realize it's nine o'clock, and my schoolbooks are scattered on my desk in front of me, and all my homework is done.

Even more strange, there's an old iron key on the corner of the desk, on top of a receipt from

Mr. Hubbard's antique shop. From yesterday.

The trouble is, I don't remember doing any of it.

It feels like a dream. When I try to think back over the night, I can only catch snippets. A question Dad asked me. A paragraph in my history book. The soap on my hands as I did the dishes.

It all feels like it happened to somebody else.

What happened at school also feels like it happened to somebody else.

I remember Melvin trying to take my ring. I remember grabbing his hand.

I remember leaving bruises.

But no . . . that can't be right.

I'm not violent.

I don't get angry.

And yet . . .

I also remember how good it felt, in those brief moments—the surge of righteous anger, the *strength*. I remember how scared Melvin and Gabby were when they looked at me.

I remember how amazing it felt to be the one doing the scaring, rather than the one being afraid.

"What is happening to me?" I whisper. I shake my

head, trying to clear the images. They filter away, like dirt down a drain, and once more that calmness reappears.

Nothing is happening.

Nothing is wrong.

21

Again I dream I am back in the Manor.

I walk through the front doors, my heels clicking on the freshly polished marble floor. Every inch of the grand entryway sparkles in the electric light. Every inch of this place is new. And yet an air already envelops the gilded frames and carpeted stairway. An air of sadness. Of age.

A haunting.

I glance in a full-length mirror. Once, I thought myself beautiful. But now—even now, in my winter fur coat, my long hair dusted with snow, my makeup perfectly done—I feel like a monster.

I don't head toward the corridor with the locked cellar. Even though that's where I should be going. Even though I know it's where *he* wants me to go. Instead, I sweep up the grand staircase. There are tears in my eyes. Tears of frustration.

Of fear.

I make my way to the back of the manor, to one of the many rooms set aside entirely for my collection. Roman artifacts and contemporary art pieces are lovingly arranged on their pedestals, the perfect museum lighting casting them all in a gentle glow. Only a few pedestals are empty. Wooden crates with unpacked artifacts are stacked in one corner, and I head toward them, shuffling off my coat and tossing it onto a chair as I go. I instantly grab a crowbar and begin prying open the crate nearest me, even though my fingers are still cold. Outside, snow falls down in thick flakes. I nearly skidded the car twice on my way down the long, winding drive.

I should have taken the turns slower. But I had to get away.

I had to get away from town.

I started to feel the itch again, when I was in the diner in town.

> When I saw that cherubic little boy sitting in
> the booth with his parents. I know *he* saw the
> boy, too.

The crate creaks open, revealing packing straw and an intricate wooden mask. Before I can reach in and take it out, however, my ring goes ice-cold.

I freeze as well.

"You know our bargain," the young boy says behind me.

I turn, slowly, my muscles no longer my own, and face the boy who haunts me.

"They're getting suspicious," I reply. My words waver. "They know something is wrong."

His single eye snares onto me.

Benjamin hates excuses.

"I require another," Benjamin says. "And you will supply one for me."

"I . . . I can't," I say. "If they find out, they'll run me out of town. Again."

There are reasons I chose this town. This plot of

land far, far away from any major city. I'd hoped his hunger would subside if there were fewer . . . options.

I was wrong. It's only gotten worse.

Benjamin shakes his head and takes a step toward me. I'd flinch back, but he controls me as easily as I would control a puppet.

"No more excuses, Janice," Benjamin says. "You will bring me another child. That is the bargain. Otherwise . . ."

He looks to the artifacts on their pedestals. They are *my* children, my prized possessions.

They're also how I found Benjamin. Or how he found me.

"No," I beg. "Please, no."

But it's too late.

Benjamin will make his point.

I jerk up to standing. The ring burns on my finger, burns in my chest, burns like the tears streaming down my cheeks as Benjamin gestures with his tiny hand, and my own arm rises up. I still hold the crowbar.

My arm thrashes to the side, and the crowbar

smashes against a porcelain vase. My priceless vase.

And I can't do anything as it explodes in shards of ceramic.

Benjamin gestures to the other side, and my arm swings out again. The crowbar rips through a Renaissance painting.

I can't even cry out as I watch the canvas rend in two.

Benjamin drops his hand.

The crowbar falls from my fingertips. But he hasn't released me.

Not yet.

He never will. Not fully.

"Now," he says smoothly, his childish voice calm and eerie, given the horrible words that I know will spill from his lips. "You will bring me another child. The boy in the diner. The one we saw."

I look to the ring. The eye darts about.

Benjamin's eye.

Through it, he sees everything.

"Do not make me angry again, Janice," Benjamin says. "You have no idea what I am capable of."

He vanishes in a blink. I tumble to my knees as his control vanishes, too.

You have no idea what I am capable of, he warned.

But I do.

I do.

22

"Mind if I sit down?" Javier asks.

I blink and look over to him. My head is fuzzy, and there's a dull ache behind my eyes, like I haven't slept in a while.

"I thought you weren't talking to me," I say. Even my voice is rough.

"I wasn't," he says. "But then I felt bad for you sitting all alone over here. You look like a zombie, Kaden."

I finally look around. Realize the low grumble in my ears isn't just my imagination, but people.

I'm in the cafeteria.

Wait. When did I . . . ?

There's a plate of food half-eaten in front of me, and I have the faint taste of chocolate on my tongue from the brownie.

"Are you feeling okay?" Javier asks. He leans in. "You're looking a little pale. And your eyes . . ."

I blink and look away from him. Try to focus on something other than the concern on his face. Try to keep my own face calm and composed.

I can't let him know that I don't remember getting here.

I don't remember eating half my lunch.

I don't remember coming to school.

I don't even remember waking up.

Panic races through me, but then my gaze catches on the silver ring on my finger. The eye, I swear, is looking at me. And once more, that cool, calming sensation sweeps through me, and my confusion just fades.

"I feel fine," I reply. I look at him then, and smile.

Why had I been freaking out? Why had I been scared to look at him?

"Oh . . . kay," he says. "Well . . . look, I know we

both said some things we didn't mean yesterday. But I wanted to see if we could put it behind us. Because, you know, you're not the best conversationalist, but you're a lot better than Ferdinand."

It's then I notice he has the ballerina mouse sitting on his lunch tray. I laugh.

"I'll take that as a compliment," I say.

"Friends?" he asks.

I nod. "Friends."

He hesitates. "Have you heard the rumors?" he asks.

"No?" I reply. Because maybe I have—I don't remember anything from the morning, but that's probably just because I didn't sleep well.

"Jake still isn't back," Javier says quietly. "People are starting to think he ran away. Or . . . or was kidnapped."

I shrug.

I don't want to talk about Jake.

"I don't think I've ever seen Gabby so upset," Javier continues. He looks over to where Gabby and Melvin sit alone. I follow his gaze. Both of them are hunched over their meals. They look afraid.

"Serves her right," I say. I'm reminded suddenly of them chasing me into the Manor, of the threats Gabby has made over the last few years. It's about time she's the one who's scared.

"Still," Javier says. "What if there's, like, a killer on the loose?"

"In Marshall Junction? Please."

He shrugs. Starts eating his lunch.

"Want to come over tonight?" he eventually asks.

The ring goes cold.

"I can't," I find myself saying.

"Oh? Big plans?"

"You could say that."

"Well, maybe tomorrow, then."

I think I agree. I can't hear what I say, or what he replies. All I can do is look over to Gabby and Melvin.

Melvin is facing us. And he must feel my stare.

He looks up. At me.

Normally, making eye contact with him would be enough to make me panic. But I don't look away. I don't cower.

He does.

23

It's late.

I blinked, and suddenly the day was over.

I blinked, and I find myself standing here, on the sidewalk outside a house, outside *his* house. And I don't know how I got here.

And I don't *care* how I got here.

I'm here now. That's what's important.

Benjamin is hungry.

All the lights in the house are out. All save for a window along the side. I know who's in that room.

I know it isn't just Melvin.

It's enough to make me hesitate. I feel Benjamin's slight concern. *One, I can take . . .*

But it is late, and I know that everyone in the house is asleep.

My feet move me across the yard, the grass cold and wet in the late-night dew.

A small voice is screaming out in the back of my mind. Telling me to turn around. I shouldn't be here. I shouldn't be doing this. But that voice fades with every footstep.

The ring on my finger is as cold as ice and vibrating with excitement. No matter how I move my hand, the eye continues to stare at that one glowing window.

It won't break its gaze from its next victim.

I make my way over slowly. My footsteps are soft, noiseless.

Benjamin has had years of practice at not making a sound.

All the rooms in Melvin's house are on one floor, just like Jake's. It's easy to reach his window. I creep over and peer inside.

A single light glows on a desk. Melvin is fast

asleep, tangled up in blankets in his bed along the opposite wall. Gabby lies on the floor in a sleeping bag, between me and my target. The ring sparks angrily, a shock through my fingers. But it isn't going to give up just yet.

Carefully, I lift the window, grateful it isn't latched.

Slowly, catlike, I climb over the windowsill and slink inside.

Melvin's room looks just like any other boy's— there are posters on the wall of cars and bands, a TV and game system in the corner. Piles of clothes haphazardly shoved to the walls. And Melvin looks almost peaceful asleep in his bed.

I creep over, stepping gingerly around Gabby, and peer over Melvin's bed.

"It's time to wake up, Melvin," I whisper. My words are gruff. They sound like the one-eyed boy's. Like Benjamin's. "It's time to play."

"What?" he asks groggily as he slowly sits up, rubbing sleep from his eyes.

Too late, he realizes it's me.

The moment his eyes widen, the moment his lips

part to call out, I raise the ring in front of me, the eye facing him.

The ring pulses. Sparks cold electricity.

Melvin's eyes grow heavy, then close. He slumps back on the bed.

I reach under him and lift him up, draping him over my shoulder in a fireman's carry. Even though this body is small, it is strong. It will do what I tell it to.

Melvin doesn't stir as I turn around and step over Gabby. He doesn't even mumble as I slowly lower him out the window.

I slink out next to him. But as I reach up to the window to pull it back down, Gabby wakes up.

She looks over. First to Melvin's bed. Then she jolts upright and looks straight at me.

"*Shh*," I whisper, raising my hand.

Her eyes go wide then slack as the ring works its twisted magic.

She falls back to her pillow, asleep immediately.

But the act of magic, of compelling two kids at once, drains me. Melvin stirs on the grass at my feet. I crouch down and press a hand to his forehead. The ring's power seeps into him. He falls asleep in moments.

When I stand, however, my body cries out.

As does that tiny voice in the back of my head. It's louder than ever.

"This just won't do," I say to myself. I can't carry Melvin the rest of the way. Not in this state. Not without risking . . .

My eyes catch on a wheelbarrow around back.

"Well, then," I whisper. I look to Melvin. "Time to get you home."

24

"Kaden, honey," my mom calls. She knocks lightly on my door. "Kaden, are you okay?"

I grumble and roll over.

Every muscle in my body aches. Especially my shoulders and my feet. I feel like I didn't sleep at all. And how could I have, with those strange dreams? What were they again?

I hear Mom open the door.

"Kaden?"

I groan. I don't open my eyes. I just roll over and squeeze a pillow to my head.

I feel her sit down on the bed beside me.

"Are you feeling okay?" she asks. "It's nearly time for school."

I mumble something.

She pulls back the pillow and presses her hand to my forehead.

"Oh, Kaden. You're burning up. I'll call the school and tell them you're not feeling well. Can I get you anything?"

I don't answer.

I know she leaves. But I don't remember when she stood up to go.

I know because I feel the bed move again when she sits down and holds out a glass of juice.

"Here," she says. "Take this. And here's some aspirin for your head."

I manage to push myself up. I take the pills and am about to take the water when she gently holds my wrist.

"Sweetie, what did you do to your hands?"

I look.

My palms are coated in blisters, red and raw, with a few splinters stuck in my fingers.

As if I'd been pushing a wheelbarrow.

My dream floods back, along with fear.

Was that a dream?

"I'll go get some bandages," she says when I don't answer. "You go to the bathroom and clean those up."

I nod numbly as she goes. I keep staring at my palms.

Then my eyes catch on the ring band. Even though my hands are scraped raw, the ring isn't tarnished in the slightest.

Panic races through me.

Did I actually go to Melvin's last night? I thought it was a dream, only . . .

I push myself out of bed and hurry to the bathroom. Start washing my hands with hotter and hotter water.

I don't look at the ring. I keep my eyes squeezed shut. I remember what looking at it did to Gabby and Melvin.

I didn't go to Melvin's last night. That's impossible. I didn't lug him all the way to the Blood Manor. And I didn't do it to Jake, either. That wasn't me! I'd never do something like that!

And as I wash my painful hands, I try to peel off the ring as well.

It doesn't budge.

If anything, the band seems to tighten.

If I actually did take Melvin . . . if I actually did capture Jake . . . why didn't I remember before? I think back to the last few days. Any fear of the ring or what's been happening to me has been pushed out of my mind.

So why can I remember it now? Why am I able to feel fear now?

It hits me: Last night, the ring put Gabby and Melvin to sleep. Played with their memories. Maybe the ring was drained. Maybe . . .

"Why. Can't. I. Get. You. Off?" I grunt, trying to yank the ring off my finger.

"Because I'm not done with you yet," a voice says. Benjamin's voice. Right by my ear.

I freeze.

I look into the mirror.

To see the one-eyed boy standing beside me in the reflection.

He smiles evilly.

"We aren't done. Not yet. So rest up, Kaden. You'll need your strength for what you're about to do."

A cold wave washes over me.

A cold, calming wave.

I don't remember turning the water off.

I don't remember drying my hands.

I don't remember going back to my room.

I only realize I'm in my bed when Mom comes in with a roll of bandages and some ointment.

"I can do it myself," I say.

I don't know what she says.

The haze washes over me, and the rest of the day passes by in a blur.

25

"Kaden's not feeling well," I hear my dad say.

"I know," comes Gabby's voice. What's Gabby doing in my house? "But I have to see them. It's important."

"Oh . . . okay. Just, um, don't be too long."

The next thing I know, Gabby is standing by my bed. I don't even remember her coming into the room. I blink at her blearily. I've done nothing but sleep all day.

At least I haven't had any dreams.

Unless this is a dream. It has to be a dream. Gabby has no reason to be in my room. She hasn't been in here since kindergarten.

This must be a dream.

I close my eyes and nuzzle back into the pillow.

Until her hand on my shoulder shakes me awake.

"No, no sleeping," she says. "Wake up, Kaden."

She doesn't sound like her usual, angry self. She sounds scared. Which means this *must* be a dream. So I guess I'll play along with it.

"What is it?" I ask.

"Where were you?" she replies.

My fuzzy head swims even more.

"What? I was right here . . ."

"Don't play stupid," she interjects. "Where were you last night?"

My thoughts don't connect. This is such a weird dream . . .

"Answer me, Kaden!"

Her fear shocks me awake.

I blink at her a few times. Yes. She's here. In my room. And strangest of all, it looks like she's been crying.

"I don't understand," I manage. "I was here. Sleeping. What do you want from me?"

"I . . ." She shakes her head, then flops down on

the bed beside me. "I was staying over at Melvin's last night. He was worried. Worried he was going to be next . . . so I stayed over, and we went to bed, and everything was fine. But when I woke up, he was gone."

I keep my hands under the covers. She doesn't need to see the bandages. She doesn't need to wonder what they're from. Even though . . . wait, how did my hands end up covered in bandages?

"What does this have to do with me?" I ask. "I was here. Ask my parents."

She doesn't make eye contact.

"He was scared because he swore he saw you outside his window," she says. "He thought you were watching him. He thought you were going to take him next."

"What are you talking about?" I ask. "Why would I take him? *Where* would I take him? If you haven't noticed, I've spent the last few years trying to avoid you three."

She glances at me. Then looks away.

"Just tell me where you were," she says.

"I did. Here. I don't know what you want me to

say. Melvin's *huge*. And Jake's like one solid muscle. Are you really telling me you think I—what? Snuck into their rooms and dragged them away? That's ridiculous. I mean, how many times have you called me weak or laughed at me in gym because I couldn't do a pull-up?"

She swallows. And for a moment she's exactly like I remember her, exactly as she was in kindergarten— shy, nervous, quiet. The girl who used to be my friend, before she decided the only way to get through school was to become mean and make everyone else miserable.

"I had a dream," she says.

"So?"

"I dreamed I saw you in his room last night," she whispers.

I stare at her.

"It was just a dream," I say. "Dreams don't mean anything." *Don't they?*

She sighs and shakes her head and stares at the floor. Then she takes a deep breath and stands. When she looks at me again, the old Gabby is gone, replaced with her angry self.

"I know you had something to do with this," she replies. "I'm going to find him. And I'm going to stop you from ever hurting anyone again."

"I'm not hurting anyone," I say. My dreams swirl. I push them down. "The only person hurting people here is *you*."

Her eyes narrow. "There's something wrong with you, Kaden. And I'm not going to stop until I find out what it is."

Without waiting for a response, she turns and leaves.

It's only when she's gone that I realize my heart is still racing. I feel like I've gotten away with something terrible. But I haven't done anything, right? I mean, I couldn't do anything. I'm just . . . me.

My dreams slosh around in my head, blurring with reality. I look down at my hands. They're completely bandaged, two big mittens of cotton. I slowly unwrap part of one, revealing the gray-eyed ring. It stares up at me, cold and unmoving.

It's just a ring.

And Gabby was just having strange dreams.

Even if I dreamed I'd been in Melvin's room, too.

I wasn't taking anyone. I wouldn't. I couldn't.

The ring gets colder. Everything is fine. Gabby is just being Gabby. Just trying to turn me into a victim again.

Mom pokes her head in the room. "Kaden, honey? Are you okay? I've made dinner if you're hungry."

My stomach rumbles. It feels like I haven't eaten in days. Like I've run a marathon.

I get out of bed, trying not to wince at the aches shooting through my muscles, and make my way to the door. I pause when I see my reflection in the mirrored display shelves, the ones holding all my precious, useless artifacts.

I walk over. Lean in closer.

My heart flips.

My eyes.

My eyes are bloodshot. Silvery around the edges. They're normally brown, but now . . .

now they're turning gray.

The same gray as the glass eye on my finger.

26

When I get back to my room after dinner, I check my phone for the first time since yesterday.

I have a dozen messages from Javier.

All asking if I'm okay.

All asking if I heard what happened to Melvin.

I stare at my phone for a long time.

My dreams continue to churn beneath the surface. Standing outside Jake's house. Sneaking in through Melvin's window. Magically putting Gabby back to sleep with the ring's power.

A part of me wants to tell Javier I've been dreaming about the missing kids. To tell him I worry that it might *actually* be me doing those horrible acts. But that voice is small, and the more I stare at Javier's text, the quieter the voice becomes.

I'm not doing anything wrong. I've just been feeling out of it. Perfectly normal.

I set down the phone without replying.

But I can't fall asleep.

I lie in my bed, staring at the illuminated artifact displays, until way after my parents go to bed.

Despite my calm, that voice from earlier doesn't go away. It's quiet, sure, but it's still there. A worry. A question.

What if . . . ?

Finally, when it's clear that I'm not going to sleep anytime soon, I slip out of bed and make my way outside.

The night air is warm, the skies clear and the moon shining bright. The whole neighborhood is asleep. Only a few streetlamps illuminate the dark.

I grab my bike from the side of the house and ride.

My hands hurt on the handlebars, and my feet ache as I pedal, but that's almost comforting in a way. As the night air blows through my hair, it becomes harder and harder to think this is real. The soupy, humid warmth of the night, the blur of streetlamps, the trill of cicadas . . . it all feels like a dream. But the pain is enough to keep me rooted. To keep reminding me, with every pedal, with every turn, that this is real. I am awake. I am doing this.

I am me.

I bike to the outskirts of town, down a gravel road that leads me past Javier's house and toward the woods. All I can see is the faint silver glow of the moonlight on the cornfields, my tiny patch of lamplight on the gravel. All I can hear are the cicadas, and my squeaky tire, and my panting breath.

I reach the woods and turn down the tangled drive toward the Blood Manor. The closer I get, the more the dreamlike quality increases. Here, the air is cold and sticky. Here, the only light comes from my bike light.

Here, it's nearly impossible to convince myself that anything is real.

But I keep going. Until I reach the clearing and the iron gate. Between one blink and the next I am stepping through the bars. My head swims.

What am I doing here? I should go home . . .

I'm just about to turn around when I notice something on the back of my hand.

Writing.

My writing. But when did I write this?

There are only three words: *Blood Manor Cellar.*

Memory sparks.

The cellar. In my dreams, the kids have been led to the cellar. The same cellar where I found the ring.

I hesitate, my mind desperately trying to wake up as something else soothes it to sleep.

"You should go home," a voice whispers beside me.

I don't glance over.

I don't want to see Benjamin, the one-eyed ghost. But I know it's him.

Chills race down my spine.

He's right, though. I should go home.

I should . . .

As I turn and make my way back to the fence, wondering what I'm doing here in the first place, wondering why I'm dreaming about the Blood Manor again, a noise in the woods makes me hesitate.

It sounds like crashing. Racing.

A lithe, monstrous beast tearing down the drive.

Then it gets closer, and I see a light sweeping along the rubble.

A light that sweeps over me, blinding me. I shield my eyes with an arm and stumble back.

The light blinks out.

I hear something fall. A bike?

And for one brief moment, I worry that Gabby has followed me here, that she's going to finish what she started and beat me up.

But when I blink, I realize that it's worse than Gabby. Much worse.

It's Javier.

27

"What are you doing here?" we both ask at the same time.

Javier takes a hesitant step forward. I take a step back, brushing against the gate.

The ring burns cold against my hand. I don't say anything. Just stare at Javier. He eventually looks down to his feet.

"I was worried about you," he says. "I . . . I got a call from Gabby. She said she visited you. She said you didn't look like yourself."

"You're talking to Gabby now?" I ask. Anger laces my words. Gabby's my *enemy*. Why is he talking to her?

"She called me! I didn't recognize the number. Besides, she went to *your* house."

"Yeah, but—"

"I was worried about you," he interrupts. "So is she."

"She thinks I'm behind their disappearances."

"I . . . I know."

"Do *you* think that?" I ask.

Javier doesn't answer right away, which is answer enough.

"I don't know," he finally tells me. "The Kaden I know wouldn't do anything like that. But . . . why are you here, Kaden?" He gestures to the Blood Manor.

"I couldn't sleep."

"Neither could I. But that doesn't answer why you came all the way out here."

I shrug.

"How did you find me?"

"I had a hunch," he says.

Javier takes another step toward me.

"Kaden . . . what's going on? Come on, you can tell me. I'm your best friend, remember?"

I want to tell him. I want to tell him everything.

But before I can say anything, a chill washes over me. My body freezes. I can't move a muscle.

Beside me, I feel Benjamin's presence.

He's here.

And he wants Javier.

"Take him," Benjamin whispers in my ear.

"What did you say?" Javier asks. He looks confused. Wait . . . did I say that out loud?

That overwhelming calming sensation intensifies. I just want to slip away, to fade into the dream . . .

But Javier is in front of me. Javier, my best friend. And I know . . . I know what will happen if I let myself disappear. He will, too. But he won't come back.

"Run," I manage.

One word. That's all I can get out before Benjamin's grip on me intensifies.

"Kaden, what—"

The ring vibrates, a piercing pulse that nearly sends me to my knees. It ricochets through my body, makes my vision waver and fade.

"Kaden . . ." I hear. Distantly.

Then my vision goes dark, and all I hear is Benjamin's laughter.

28

"Let me go," I implore. Tears stream down my face. "Please, let me go."

Benjamin just laughs. "You know I can't do that, Janice. Not until we've finished our work. Unless . . ."

He trails off, his one eye snared at me, while the eye on my finger glares up.

Unless you wish to switch places.

I know that's the bargain.

Either I let him take over my body and become the one trapped in the ring, or I continue to . . .

Downstairs, in the cellar, I hear a kid scream out

for his mommy. More tears fill my eyes. I wipe them hastily away.

I stand in front of the bathroom mirror. I swear my bloodshot eyes have grown more silver over the past few days. With every child taken, with every child Benjamin locks away, the stronger his influence grows. But that is why he is doing this. The more kids he steals, the more of their energy he can take. The stronger he becomes. Until one day . . . one day he won't need me to be his vessel anymore.

One day he will be free to enact his revenge.

"I can't do it anymore," I want to say. I grab for the ring on my finger.

In this one brief moment of clarity, I think I might be able to do it, to pull off the ring and break free. His hold on me is normally so complete.

I grab the silver band.

But just as it begins to slide off my finger, he laughs. I know then he was simply toying with me.

The ring clamps down on my finger, along with a burst of cold electricity that drops me to my knees.

"If you can't do it anymore," Benjamin says, kneeling down in front of me, "all you need to do is say so."

The ring is cold. So cold. And I know it is draining more than my heat and willpower. It's draining my essence.

He needs me to act as his hand. So long as I'm alive, so long as I wear the ring, he can compel me to do his dirty work. There is only one other option: I die, and let him take over my body. But then he can do anything he wants, anywhere he wants. At least while I'm alive, I have a small amount of control over what he does. Until I've completed his work. Then, nothing can stop him.

"Help us, please, somebody!" screams a child in the cellar.

I shudder.

No help is coming. We are too far away from town for that.

"I'll never let you take over my body," I say. "But I can't let you hurt anyone else."

Benjamin smiles his cold, terrible smile, and stands.

"We will see about that," he says. "Unlike you, I have all the time in the world."

Then, in a blink, he is gone.

I flop back on the tiles momentarily, breathing in deep.

I know he is right. I know that, soon, the townspeople will grow more suspicious. They will come looking for me. They will find me, and the kids captured in the basement. And they will kill me. And then . . . and then, Benjamin will leapfrog to the next body, and the horrible cycle will happen again.

Soon, Benjamin will be back. He'll take over my mind, and I'll forget who I am. For now, though, I'm just Janice Hoffweller, collector of ancient artifacts . . . and discoverer of cursed rings.

I push myself to stand. At least, while I am myself, I can try to clean away my smeared makeup.

Except, when I stare in the mirror, it isn't me staring back. Nor is it Benjamin. It's a young child. A child with shoulder-length hair and strange clothes.

Me . . . I'm looking at me. Kaden.

I shake my head. The reflection blurs, and one moment I see the figure of Janice Hoffweller, the next I see Kaden. They are both me. In this vision, in this dream, we are trapped just the same.

"I tried to warn you," she says through my lips.

"I tried to get you to leave. To give the ring back. But you wouldn't listen . . ."

I . . . I didn't mean . . . I think, but I can't make my lips move.

"Now it's too late." Tears fill her—my—eyes.

She holds up her hands. Her scarred, bleeding hands. Mangled, save for the silver ring we both share. The eye stares at me.

It knows.

Then, with a horrible wail, she slams my hand into the mirror.

Glass shatters.

So, too, does the dream.

29

I wake up, and I am in the hallway at school.

For a split second I think I must be dreaming again, because how in the world did I get here? Last I remember, I was in bed. Or, wait . . . was I at the Manor? And Javier . . . No, no, that was all a dream, too, just like this. Because everyone is walking toward the exit, which means this is the end of a school day, and I don't remember it at all.

Then someone bumps into me, knocking me against a locker and making me drop my books.

Yup. Definitely really here.

I shake my head, trying to get my blurred thoughts

to settle as I bend down to grab my books, when I see someone's boots stop in front of me.

Gabby.

She kneels down in front of me and picks up a book.

I fully expect her to hit me with it, but she just looks at me nervously.

"How are you feeling?" she asks.

And it's such an innocent question, such a *nice* question, that I almost pinch myself. This *has* to be a dream.

"What?" I ask.

She swallows and looks away. "You've been gone a few days. All weekend. I tried visiting but your parents wouldn't let me in. And, well, Javier's been missing. I thought maybe you were worried."

"What?" I repeat, only louder this time.

Her words slam into me.

I've been out all weekend. I don't remember . . . I don't . . .

And Javier.

"You . . . you didn't know?"

I shake my head. "He . . . what?"

She doesn't answer right away. Instead, she looks around and then helps me get back up. She doesn't say another word until she's led me outside and around the school, to a patch of playground that's completely empty.

"Kaden, I think something terrible is going on," she says.

I don't know what to say, so I just stay silent.

"Melvin and Jake went missing last week," she says. "And then you got sick. And then Javier went missing. And . . . Kaden, you don't look like yourself. Not at all."

As if to accentuate her point, she holds up her phone in selfie mode so I can see my reflection.

She's right.

There are dark shadows under my eyes, and my irises are more silver than ever. I look like I haven't slept in weeks. But what else could I have been doing? What else . . .

A dream swirls through my muddied thoughts.

A dream of me standing at the gates of the Blood Manor.

A dream of Javier confronting me.

A dream of me raising the ring, of letting Benjamin's magic overpower him . . .

"Javier," I gasp. I look at Gabby. "I think I know where he is. Where they all are."

Gabby nods, and together we head to the Manor.

30

I tell Gabby everything as we pedal into the forest. Despite the chill air, I'm sweating. I don't know if it's from fear or from the woozy sensation rolling through my limbs. I want to fall back asleep. I want to just sink . . .

But every time I feel that, I think about Javier.

Remember who you are, I tell myself. *Remember who needs you.*

Gabby doesn't say anything the entire time. Not when I say the ring is possessed, not when I say the ghost inhabiting it is compelling me to do what it compelled Janice Hoffweller to do: steal children.

I don't want to believe Benjamin would be able to make me do such a thing. I couldn't. I wouldn't.

But if I did . . . Javier, Melvin, and Jake have to be okay. Trapped, but okay.

I can't allow myself to think otherwise, because then I'll just collapse into a puddle and cry.

But that also makes me wonder why Benjamin isn't compelling me *now*. If he was controlling me all weekend, why stop now? Did he get tired? Bored?

I look down to the ring on my hand. It still burns like ice, and the moment I try to take it off, it clamps down so tight I bite back a yelp. The ring isn't going anywhere, which means Benjamin hasn't, either.

"I can't believe I've been out of it for so long," I whisper. "The entire weekend . . ." That alone scares me as much as the thought of what I might have done to Javier. I don't remember *anything*.

"Well, you didn't get up to anything exciting, if that's what you're worried about," she says, glancing over at me. "I was, um, pulling a stakeout in front of your place ever since Javier went missing."

"You were stalking me?"

"You were the only suspect," she replies. "And it's

a good thing I did, too. Since apparently I was right. But yeah, you didn't leave the house. I went to check on you once and your parents said you were sleeping, and they'd called a doctor but there didn't seem to be anything wrong. I was surprised when you showed up to school today."

Me too, I think.

But before I can wonder anymore, we reach the driveway leading to the Blood Manor. Fresh sweat breaks out across my skin.

I swear I smell woodsmoke the closer we get.

I blink, and we are both standing right in front of the Manor's burnt entry, and Gabby is saying something—

"—in here?"

"What?" I ask. How did we get here already?

"Are you sure they're in here?" she asks. She looks at me strangely. Like she's nervous. Nervous I might be the dangerous one, out of the two of us.

I nod. The compulsion to sleep is stronger than ever, and it gets worse with every step we take past the wrought iron fence. It feels like I was just here yesterday. It feels like I haven't been here for years.

I walk as if in a dream. Gabby holds her phone in

one hand, and I clutch the ring on my finger as if I could keep in the evil. My blood is pounding, and if I move my head too quickly my vision blurs, just a little, like everything is a breath away from becoming fog. So I don't move my head. I don't want to fall asleep again.

I don't trust what I'll do. Not when we're this close to the source of all this evil.

"Lead on," Gabby says when we reach the front door.

I nod, and while she uses her phone as a flashlight, I lead us down the marble hallway, toward the cellar at the end. Everything is silent. Dead silent. And I start to fear the worst.

What if I *did* hurt Javier and the rest? If they're locked away in here, shouldn't they be crying out?

We turn a corner.

Gabby's light glides over the hall.

And illuminates the ghostly form of Janice Hoffweller.

31

Gabby screams out.

If I wasn't so out of it, I would scream as well.

Instead, I stare at the ghostly form of Miss Hoffweller—her aura of gray hair, her ragged dress, her sunken face—and for a brief, horrible moment I feel myself *flip*.

Suddenly, I am the one floating in the hall, staring at the two children who have entered my domain.

Then I blink and I'm back in my body, and the whole hallway rolls as the woozy sensation comes back.

"You shouldn't be here!" the ghost wails.

Any normal kid would turn and run. But Gabby

doesn't. She just balls up her fists and glowers at the ghost, as if in defiance.

"Are you the one who stole all those kids?" she demands. "Are you the one taking over Kaden?"

The ghost shakes her head.

"No," I say for the ghost. "She . . . I mean, yes. It wasn't her. It was Benjamin. He controlled her. He made her do those horrible things."

"As he is controlling you," Miss Hoffweller replies.

"He's gone now," I say. She interrupts before I can go further.

"Benjamin is never gone," she says. "The moment you put on the ring, you are his . . . forever."

"Then where is he?" I ask. "Why am I . . . ?" But I can't figure out how to say it—*Why am I in control of my own body? Why don't I feel him? Why isn't he taking over?*

She seems to understand the question.

"Benjamin enjoys toying with his hosts," she says. "It brings him as much pleasure as collecting his victims."

"Then how do we get rid of him?" Gabby asks. And it strikes me how strange this is, the two of us—once enemies—talking to a ghost. But I still feel like I'm dreaming, so it all makes perfect sense. "You did it once."

"At the cost of my life . . ." Janice replies.

She looks at me, and even though her visage is terrifying, her eyes soften with sadness.

"And even then," she continues, "it did not seal away his evil for long."

"How?" I ask. "How did you do it?"

She glides forward.

Places a transparent hand on the ring.

Cold and pain shoot through me, and when I can see again, I'm no longer in the ruins of the Manor.

32

Quiet.

Everything is quiet.

Terribly so.

The winter storm outside has died down. The fire in the hearth has gone out.

The quiet suffocates me.

A sob rips from my lungs, the only sound in this abysmal silence. This horrible emptiness.

"I can't do this anymore," I whisper to the walls.

I look around the room. I stand in one of my collection displays, surrounded by all the artifacts I've collected over the years. Once, they were my pride and joy. Now, they mean nothing. Not in the light of the horrible things I've done.

I look down to the ring stuck forever on my finger.

If not for that collection, I never would have discovered this. This ring, in the bottom of a trunk at an old estate sale. I'd known then that I had to have it.

If only I had known that it was the *ring* that had to have *me*.

Since I put it on, I haven't been myself. The ghost with one eye, the boy who called himself Benjamin, had taken over. Slowly, at first, and then more viciously, voraciously, as his appetite grew.

I can only feed him so much.

I came here, to the middle of nowhere, in hopes he would be sated. In hopes he would quiet down. Or go away.

He will never go away.

I once more grab the ring on my finger and try to rip it off. I hold back a scream as my knuckles crack, as my skin rips, but the ring refuses to budge. Tears stream down my face. I need to get this off.

Before Benjamin wakes from his temporary slumber.

He always slumbers after I've brought him some-one new and he's feasted on their sadness, growing stronger from their misery.

Just the thought makes me cry out in agony.

I can't do this again.

I can't let him do this to me again.

My eyes sweep over my collection. Hoping to find something that will help me break this curse.

I catch sight of a ceremonial dagger in a display case, sitting in a lacquered black box. I look down to my finger.

A terrible idea crosses my mind.

Before I can stop myself, I go over to the case and—with only a moment's regret—slam my fist into the glass display. The casing shatters, cutting my knuckles, but I don't feel it. Soon, it won't matter.

For a moment, I consider doing it here. In this room.

But this is on the upper levels. If I die, someone will come and discover me. Discover *it*.

I can't risk that happening.

There is only one place in this cursed manor where I can hide it forever.

The one place I never want to step foot in again.

I grab the box and head to the cellar.

I walk in a daze, but it's less the effect of Benjamin and more my own disbelief. At what I must do. At what I *will* do.

My hand shakes as I unlock the padlock on the door.

My knees tremble as I close the cellar door behind me.

As I walk down the cold concrete steps.

To the final door. The door with the crystal skull knob.

"I wouldn't do that, if I were you," comes Benjamin's voice. I turn, and he stands halfway up the stairs, more solid than ever before. His single eye glares at me.

I don't respond. I know I don't have much time. He may be tired after feeding on sorrows, but he is stronger than he ever was. As I stare at him, I realize he is less transparent than usual. He is almost flesh again.

He is almost free.

I rip open the door and run into the room.

I know doors won't stop Benjamin, but I slam it shut behind me.

I've already hidden the children in the garden shed. There, wrapped in blankets, huddled against the cold, they sleep. A dreamless slumber I couldn't force any of them to wake from. Benjamin was still feeding on their essence, still growing stronger as they fell weak. I had to get them out of the house.

I had to save them.

I have no idea how Benjamin will respond to my betrayal, but I know it won't be pleasant. Not if the ruined artifacts of mine were any indication. I couldn't let the children suffer my failures. Not anymore.

I set the lacquered box on a pedestal, a plinth that should have held a priceless artifact, and not this horrible tragedy.

"You know what will happen if you remove the ring," Benjamin growls.

I feel his compulsion over me grow.

Feel him try to wrestle back control.

"You'll never control me," I say. "Ever again."

And in one swift movement, I raise the dagger

and slice

off

my finger.

I scream in pain and am rewarded with an even harsher agony.

It starts in my hand, a cold burn, and spreads up my arm.

Fire.

Flames race up my dress, crackle on my skin.

Flames billow up around me, burning me, sweeping out in the halls of the house, consuming everything I've spent my life collecting.

I cry out.

But Benjamin doesn't. He isn't angry. And as the world burns away, I worry this had all been a mistake.

Because as I cry, he just stares at me, flames flickering through him.

And I know, somehow, that I have failed.

33

I stagger back and nearly fall over. Gabby catches me.

"What . . ." I stammer. "What was that?"

"How I got rid of him," the ghost of Janice Hoffweller says. She holds up her hand to reveal only four fingers. "But clearly, not forever."

My mind reels. So the fire started to punish Miss Hoffweller for removing the ring. That's what burned the whole place down around her. She did it to protect the town. To save the children. She did it to prevent Benjamin from taking anyone else.

Only . . .

"I have to save them," I say. I look to Gabby.

"Come on, I know where they are."

"You mustn't go down there!" the ghost says. "He will compel you! And when he does . . ."

But I don't stand around to listen. The moment she says it, I see the eyeball in the ring twitch.

Benjamin knows. And I can tell from the cold that seeps through my veins that he is coming back.

I dart forward, and the ghostly form of Janice Hoffweller disappears. Gabby and I run down the hall, heading toward the cellar.

"What did you see?" Gabby asks. "How do we stop it?"

"When we get in there," I gasp to Gabby, "you have to get them out. Don't wait for me. Just take them and leave!"

If I can get them clear of the house . . . if I can hold Benjamin off . . .

"What about you?" Gabby asks.

"I'll be right behind you," I lie.

It's silent when we reach the cellar door, but I am not surprised: Benjamin is drawing on their energy, forcing them to sleep while he grows stronger.

I grab the old iron key in my pocket and fumble

with it in the padlock. Memories swirl through me, distant as dreams: me, buying the lock from Mr. Hubbard's antique store, replacing the old padlock here with one I could close. Whistling as I locked it behind every new victim lured to the chamber within. Including Javier.

My heart races as we rip open the cellar door and thunder down the steps.

Everything is a blur. I feel the compulsion swelling within me, trying to drag me down, trying to put me to sleep, but I fight it. I won't be Benjamin's tool. Not any longer.

Gabby gets to the final door first and yanks it open. This door never needed a lock. Benjamin's power ensured that no kids would try to escape from here—he only needed to keep outsiders from finding them.

Inside, Melvin and Jake and Javier are on the floor, sound asleep.

"Quickly," Gabby says. "Help me carry them."

I run over to Javier, who mumbles in his sleep. Gabby struggles beside me. Without Benjamin's strength running through me, I don't stand a chance of lifting any of them up.

Behind me, I hear someone laugh.

Benjamin.

My blood goes cold.

So, too, does the ring.

Gabby notices that I stop moving.

"Come on!" she urges. "We have to hurry."

She doesn't hear Benjamin's laughter.

I feel my lips quirk into a smile as the coldness spreads through me. As my muscles cease to obey me.

"Did you really think it would be that easy?" I hear myself say.

Then Benjamin takes over, and all I see next is darkness.

34

The world comes back into focus in a series of slow blinks.

Blink.

I am looking over at Javier, who is sound asleep beside me.

Blink.

I stare at Gabby, who sits against the wall across from me, her eyes fluttering slowly, as if fighting off sleep.

Blink.

Benjamin stands before me. Smiling.

I struggle back, but I can't move. Benjamin's control over me is absolute.

"You thought you had it all figured out," he says. "But I am one step ahead of you. Always."

"Why?" I ask. "Why are you doing this?"

"Revenge," he says. His smile slips. "When I was alive, all my classmates made fun of me for having a glass eye. For being different. Then my parents and I died in a fire, and rather than mourn us, some collector stole my eye and made it into a ring! Little did they know, that very ring would help me get my revenge. Soon, I won't need it. I've grown stronger. And once I've fed on the fear and energy of these four, I won't need to haunt you through that ring any longer. I'll be human once more!"

His smile turns wicked. The eyeball on the ring rotates. It looks to Gabby, who seems to be winning in her fight against slumber.

"You made this so easy, Kaden. I didn't think you were gullible enough to play along. To think I'd let you go. To think I'd let you betray me like that horrible woman did. No. You led the final child I need right to me. I knew she was the one, but she was too strong, too suspicious. I couldn't bring her here like I had all the rest. I had to let you do it on your own. And you did marvelously."

No, I think. But it makes a horrible sense. I'd wondered why Benjamin had let me free, why I had been able to move after an entire weekend of being blacked out. It wasn't because I'd escaped, or because he'd grown tired. It was because he had laid a trap, and I had walked right into it.

"Now," Benjamin says, "I think it's time to begin. Say goodbye to your friends, Kaden. And your body. Because once I'm through with them, I'll drain you, and then . . . I'll be free."

35

Benjamin doesn't move, but he forces me to.

My limbs jerk into motion, and I get to my knees and shuffle over to Javier.

No, I scream inside my head, even though my lips don't move. *No, please!*

"Let's make this fun," Benjamin says. "Let's hear him as he screams."

Javier's eyes flutter open.

"Kaden!" he yelps. "Kaden, please, don't do this."

I can't do anything. I have no control. No control as my body moves of its own accord, as my hands reach out and touch his neck. Javier's pulse is hot and frantic beneath my fingers.

No! I scream.

Benjamin just laughs.

As Benjamin tries to tighten my hands, I resist with everything I have.

"Kaden!" Javier gasps.

I want to stop. I want to stop more than anything I've ever wanted in my life.

Javier looks straight into my eyes.

"This isn't you," he manages. "Remember who you are."

Pain shoots through me. But this pain has nothing to do with the ring, or with the ghost controlling me.

The ache is my own.

Because Javier is right.

This isn't me.

All my life, I've had to defend myself from those around me, those who didn't understand me—how I dressed, how I acted, what I liked. I was always the outcast. Except around Javier. Javier, who always accepted me. Javier, who always knew precisely who I was, even when I wasn't so sure.

Javier. My best friend.

You know who you are.

I am not Benjamin. I am not Benjamin's toy.

The ache inside me burns. I am not willing to succumb to Benjamin. I'm not willing to become a monster like him.

My knuckles crack as I force them open. As Benjamin screams out at my side, "No! What are you doing?"

"You can't control me," I force my lips to say. I let go of Javier's neck, even though it feels like pushing through concrete.

Javier slumps back on the ground.

I stand and face the ghost that tried to consume me.

"I know who I am, and you can never change that. You can never make me be what I am not. And I. Am not. Your puppet."

Benjamin stomps up and howls, but now, he is the one who is helpless.

I feel him try to compel me, feel the ache as my muscles constrict, as I fight against myself. But my resolve is too strong. I refuse to be under his control any longer. He has pushed me too far, and I won't go any further. I will not hurt my friend.

With jerky movements, I reach down and

> yank
>
> off
>
> the
>
> ring.

Benjamin screams.

I throw the ring to the floor with all my might.

Silver hits concrete. The moment it does, the glass eye falls out of the ring and rolls away.

Benjamin vanishes in a whirl of dust.

The moment he's gone, I drop to my knees. I feel like I've run a hundred miles, like I couldn't move another muscle. But my body is mine. Mine. And there is still work to be done.

I struggle over and wrap Javier in a huge hug.

"Welcome back," he whispers into my ear. "I missed you."

"Me too," I say. "Me too."

Epilogue

"You're sure you want to get rid of all this?" Mr. Hubbard asks, looking up over the boxes I've unloaded from the car.

"Positive," I say. "I've had enough of collecting other people's things."

Mr. Hubbard grumbles something to himself. I don't catch it, but it's probably some mix of *I told you so* and also *Now I have to resell all this*. He's already unpacked a few boxes and spread out the contents on the register desk, with little tags labeled in his shaky handwriting stating the object and its cost.

"What do you think this is all worth?" Javier asks. He drops the final box at Mr. Hubbard's feet.

"I'm not certain," Mr. Hubbard replies. "It will take a few days to price everything."

"That's okay," I say.

"Until then," Javier says. "Mind if I use your restroom for free?"

Mr. Hubbard nods grumpily and waves Javier toward the restroom.

"Some people never change," Mr. Hubbard says when Javier is out of earshot.

"Nope," I say, and grin.

After rescuing Javier and Gabby and Jake and Melvin, we didn't have some big coming-together moment. Jake and Melvin have avoided me since, and even though Gabby no longer picks on me, it's clear she isn't ready to try being my friend. I guess I can't blame her.

As for the Blood Manor . . . I haven't gone back. But I've heard rumors. Rumors that it's started to collapse in on itself. That soon, it will be nothing more than a pile of rocks and brambles.

Good.

Benjamin is gone, and his ring broken, buried beneath all the rubble of the Blood Manor. Hopefully, now, no one else will fall under his spell.

While waiting for Javier, I slowly peruse the shelves. I'm not looking for anything anymore. After the ring, the last thing I want is to acquire anyone else's past. You never know what sort of price tag is attached.

But still, I wander the aisles, wondering vaguely if I can find a companion for Javier's taxidermy mouse, Ferdinand.

I hear the door open, and another customer comes in. I tune them out as Mr. Hubbard greets them.

After what seems like forever, Javier comes over.

"Ready?" he asks.

I nod.

We make our way to the exit and pass by the customer and Mr. Hubbard, who is ringing up her purchase.

"We'll be back after school tomorrow!" I say.

Mr. Hubbard just waves. "Don't get into any trouble," he says.

"We won't," Javier promises.

Halfway out the door, my breath catches. My blood freezes.

From the corner of my eye, I thought I saw what Mr. Hubbard was packing up for the customer. But no. It couldn't have been. It's still in the basement. I know I left it there.

I could have sworn the artifact he was wrapping in a tiny box was a gray glass eye.

Acknowledgments

I count myself very lucky to have grown up surrounded by friends and family who allowed me to explore and discover who I was, without judgment or bias. Finding yourself is the process of a lifetime, but it is so much easier when you're supported from the very start. So, my first and most heartfelt thanks goes to my parents and friends. Thank you for letting me be, well, *me*.

This book, though close to my heart, fought me every step of the way (it turns out, writing a book about becoming possessed is *very* difficult in first-person POV). So my deepest gratitude goes to my editor, David Levithan, for his insight and support. And patience.

To Jana Haussmann and the entire Fairs team, for their enthusiasm and excitement with every new release. It has been the honor of a lifetime to work with Scholastic, and to see these books finding the readers who need them most.

Which . . . my final thanks to you, dear reader, for your amazing letters and voracious love of words. You keep me going. Stay hungry. Stay passionate.

Stay you.

Read more from

K. R. Alexander...

if you dare

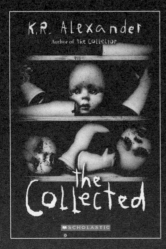

SCHOLASTIC and associated logos
are trademarks and/or registered
trademarks of Scholastic Inc.

📖 SCHOLASTIC
scholastic.com

ALEXANDER-COLLECTOR